Kathleen grew up in Potterspury, a small rural village in West Northamptonshire, eventually moving with her family to Northampton. Kathleen has always loved books ever since reading her first novel at ten years of age, Kathleen also had the desire to view the world, travelling to Australia, where she lived for several years. Returning to Northampton, Kathleen was employed within the banking world, whilst also raising two children, who are now adults and Kathleen's pride and joy.

There are two people I would like to dedicate this book to,

Firstly,

To my dad, Arthur Grant. Without him, I wouldn't be the person I am today.

Thank you, Dad, for your loving ways and guidance throughout my life,

Love you forever.

And, to my father-in-law, Eric, who is sadly no longer with us. Eric and I shared our passion for books and spent many happy hours discussing our favourite ones.

Eric will always be forever in my thoughts and hearts.

Kathleen E Grant

THE MISSING CHILD

AUSTIN MACAULEY PUBLISHERS
LONDON • CAMBRIDGE • NEW YORK • SHARJAH

Copyright © Kathleen E Grant 2025

The right of Kathleen E Grant to be identified as author of this work has been asserted by the author in accordance with sections 77 and 78 of the Copyright, Designs and Patents Act 1988.

All rights reserved. No part of this publication may be reproduced, stored in a retrieval system, or transmitted in any form or by any means, electronic, mechanical, photocopying, recording, or otherwise, without the prior permission of the publishers.

Any person who commits any unauthorised act in relation to this publication may be liable to criminal prosecution and civil claims for damages.

This is a work of fiction. Names, characters, businesses, places, events, locales, and incidents are either the products of the author's imagination or used in a fictitious manner. Any resemblance to actual persons, living or dead, or actual events is purely coincidental.

A CIP catalogue record for this title is available from the British Library.

ISBN 9781037108624 (Paperback)
ISBN 9781037108631 (ePub e-book)

www.austinmacauley.com

First Published 2025
Austin Macauley Publishers Ltd®
1 Canada Square
Canary Wharf
London
E14 5AA

20250804

I would like to thank my husband, Tim, for his encouragement in my writing and for his continued support.

Thank you, My Tim.

Chapter 1

Patrick stirred from his sleep and woke up. He smiled to himself as it was his big day here at last; he was 11 years old.

It was Saturday, 6 April 1948. He bounded down the stairs still in his pyjamas and burst into the kitchen, where his mum Sarah was busily preparing breakfast. Sarah looked at her son with affection, and he looked so much like his father.

With his slim build, sandy hair and brown eyes although their personalities were the opposite of each other. "Hello, darling, happy birthday," she said and promptly gave him a kiss. Patrick glanced at the breakfast table where he could see a birthday card and a present.

He read his birthday card and opened his present, where he found some coloured pencils, a sketch pad and to his surprise, some gumdrops.

He thanked his mum, ate his breakfast of eggs on toast in double quick time and then dashed back up to his room to get dressed. With a wave to his mum, he rode off on his bike to see his granddad, who lived on the other side of Stony Stratford.

He couldn't wait to tell his granddad about his new pencils and sketch pad. Thomas Bryant was standing by his garden gate waiting for Patrick.

"Hello, Granddad! Look what mum gave me for my birthday." Thomas knew of course, but pretended to show surprise.

"Well, well," he said, and ruffled Patrick's hair, "come inside and see what I have for your birthday." Patrick walked into the living room and there stood an easel.

An easel! Patrick who loved to draw and paint, could hardly believe his eyes. "Oh, Granddad, thank you."

Granddad told him, "I've been making that easel for a few weeks now, and had it hidden in my shed until today." Patrick wanted to attach some paper and start to draw straight away.

"Now, don't you worry about getting the easel home, lad. Mr Pearce has offered to take it home for you, so long as I provide him with a dozen eggs, that is."

Patrick couldn't thank his granddad enough. He was so pleased with the easel he had always wanted one.

Together, they left the living room and went into the garden, walking to the bottom of the garden where the chicken coop was kept.

As usual, the chickens heard them approach. Patrick went inside the coop where the chickens gathered around him pecking at his socks and shoes. This was ticklish, making him laugh.

He gave them their feed, and then investigated the nesting boxes, for some freshly laid eggs. He carefully placed the eggs into Granddad's basket.

As he stepped out of the coop, he was grinning from ear to ear. "Look, Granddad! They've laid seven eggs. We very nearly have a whole dozen for Mr Pearce, and then he really won't mind taking my easel home for me."

Thomas affectionally ruffled Patrick's hair. "Of course, he won't mind, lad. Now, come on! We have other gardening chores to do; we need to get the carrot seeds in."

Thomas had a large corner plot with his end of a terraced house, which suited him just fine. The two of them walked over to the vegetable patch. Whilst Thomas made long troughs in the soil, Patrick followed along placing the carrot seeds into the soil.

Together, they covered up the seeds, and Patrick gave them plenty of water. Once that was all done, it was time for a nice cup of tea, along with a glass of milk for Patrick. All too soon, it was time for Patrick to go home for his lunch.

Thomas hoped his son-in-law, Patrick's father, Sargent Simon Smithers as he liked to be known would at least say something nice to Patrick today, especially as today was his birthday. He was a boy to be proud of. He loved this grandson of his with all his heart, Thomas waved to him from his garden gate. Patrick waved back as best as he could whilst riding his bike home.

As Patrick peddled back home towards Church Street, he was thinking of the nice morning he had spent with his granddad. He pushed his bike down the side of his house and left it leaning against the wall. Then, he went through the back door and into the kitchen. He was looking forward to telling his mum all about the easel that Granddad had made for him.

"Mum! Mum! Where are you? Granddad has made me an easel, and Mr and Mrs Pearce are going to bring it home for me."

Then he realised his father was home. He could smell his cigarette smoke from the kitchen. Patrick's heart sank; he tried very hard not to show the fear he felt for his father, which wasn't easy.

Sargent Simon Smithers liked to be feared, it made him feel powerful, which was probably accepted in the army, but he wasn't in the army anymore.

With dread, Patrick went into the living room. His father was reading his newspaper. He looked over the top and said, "So, this is the 11-year-old who likes to spend his time scribbling."

Patrick bit his lip and looked down at the floor. "Look up when I'm speaking to you."

He looked up, but couldn't say anything; his father put his paper down and stood up.

His fists were clenched; Patrick stiffened waiting for the blow. His father could be very unpredictable and often hit him, especially when his mum wasn't at home. This time, though, he just glared at him.

"I would rather you showed some boyish ways, and played a sport instead of scribbling."

Patrick looked up, and said, "I do play sports at school, and I'm going to join the tennis club soon."

"Now I've heard it all, tennis and scribbling; you're a weakling boy."

He pushed his face close to Patrick's face, telling him he was like a girl!

Patrick bowed his head, but didn't dare move; he stood very still almost to attention.

"Now, go and fetch your mother. She's gone next door measuring up for bloody curtains again."

He was relieved his father hadn't hit him and dashed next door to fetch his mum. Mary, the next-door neighbour, was smiling as she opened the door to Patrick.

"Goodness! Your mum is clever making curtains like she does, and helping me to hang them up as well, I'm so pleased with them!"

Mary took him by the hand into the living room, showing him her new curtains. He hadn't any idea about curtains but agreed how nice they looked.

Patrick then told Mary all about his birthday presents, and helping his granddad in the garden. Before they left, Mary gave Patrick some biscuits for his birthday. He thanked her very much.

All three chatted for a while longer before saying goodbye; Patrick followed his mum back into their own house next door. Simon was waiting for them. "You took your time, and I hope she's paid you well for those infernal curtains."

Sarah said nothing; she could see the mood he was in.

"Right! Patrick! Your mother and I have something to tell you."

Sarah looked at this husband of hers, and wished he could be kind just for once, just once!

She turned towards Patrick and smiled. "You are going to have a new baby brother or sister, in a few months' time."

Patrick also smiled; he already knew about the baby. His mum had told him. His father was watching him, making him feel uncomfortable. However, Patrick managed to smile and say how pleased he was.

It was Sunday, the day after Patrick's birthday, Instead of waking up happy, he was worried and wondered if his father was at home, or had he gone out. He got dressed before going down the stairs, in case his father was at home.

His father didn't allow him downstairs wearing pyjamas, but to his relief, it was just his mum Sarah in the kitchen.

"Good morning, Patrick. It's toast today with your milk." Sarah could see that Patrick was anxious, and laid a hand on his shoulder.

"Your father has had his breakfast, and gone out to see someone, and then he's going to the George."

Patrick relaxed. In fact, they both relaxed and smiled at each other. Although they both knew his father could be even more difficult, after going to the George.

He asked, "Would it be alright if he went to see Robert after breakfast?"

Robert and Patrick had been friends since they started school together.

"We're going fishing down by the stream," he said.

"Of course, you can, but don't get all wet and muddy, like you did the time before."

"But, Mum! I just slipped on the muddy bank last time!" Sarah smiled at him. "Well, try not to slip this time, because later this afternoon, we are going to your granddads."

Patrick collected his fishing things from the garden shed, which had all been made by his granddad. Then he set off for Robert's house. Together, the two boys walked towards the stream.

Their so-called fishing nets were made of a pair of Granddad's old socks, held together by a piece of wire and tied to a long cane. Robert had some empty jam jars to put the fish inside, if they caught any that was.

Both boys sat by the stream and carefully lowered their fishing nets into the water below. They sat as still and quiet as they could, both hoping to be the first to catch a fish. Robert was the lucky one; he caught two sticklebacks one after the other. Patrick still hadn't caught anything, when suddenly a small minnow swam straight into his net!

They gently put the fish they had caught into the waiting jam jars, holding the jars up to the light to admire their catch. They stayed by the stream for a while longer but didn't catch any more fish.

Robert said, "Come on, Patrick, let's go for a paddle."

They quickly threw off their socks and plimsoles, and slowly stepped into the water, gasping and laughing at the same time, as it was so very cold.

"It's freezing," said Patrick. The water was so much colder than they both thought it would be. However, after a while, they soon got used to the cold water and were splashing with each other and laughing at the same time. Their laughter was heard by some nearby ducks, who flew off in a flurry of feathers.

Later that same afternoon, all three were sitting in some old deckchairs in Granddad's garden. They were enjoying the early spring sunshine and each other's company. Patrick was telling them all about going fishing with Robert, and what sort of fish they had caught.

Smiling, Sarah said, "And have you told your granddad how wet you were when you came home."

Patrick looked a bit sheepish, especially as they enjoyed splashing about in the stream. "Boys will be boys," said Granddad, as he reached across and ruffled his hair.

Granddad then pointed to his fruit trees. "Just look at the blossom that's starting to appear on my fruit trees, that's all down to early spring. We will have plenty of lovely fruit to eat this year, that's for sure." Patrick looked up at the blossom and agreed with his granddad.

He then pointed out the vegetable patch to his mum so she could see where they had planted the carrot seeds.

Patrick asked his granddad if he could go inside for his drawing things. Granddad always kept plenty of paper and pencils for him. Patrick thought it would be nice to draw his mum and granddad whilst they were sitting in the garden.

Whilst Patrick had gone into the house, Thomas turned to Sarah, and asked, "How are things at home?"

Thomas had a dislike of his son-in-law. He just couldn't understand him, and why he acted so disinterested in Patrick.

Thomas held Sarah's gaze, and said, "I just hate to see the worry on Patrick's face whenever his father's name is mentioned, or when it's time for him to leave here, and go home. It troubles me, Sarah."

She could feel tears beginning to well up in her eyes; she loved this dear old dad of hers and was ashamed to think of him so troubled. She was thinking of what to say that would put his mind at rest.

She stroked her rounded tummy. "I'm hoping when the baby's born, things will settle down." Although she knew Simon wasn't keen on another child. Thomas also knew and couldn't understand why that was, any more than Sarah could, as a child is a wonderful gift to have.

At that moment, Patrick appeared again from the house. He settled down on the grass in front of them crossed his legs, and began to draw. It made them both smile, to see his tongue peeping out in concentration. His mum and granddad talked about this and that, whilst he was drawing, enjoying the tranquillity of the afternoon, and each other's company as they usually did.

After a while, Patrick held up his drawing for them to see. He had even added himself into the picture, so all three were together.

"My goodness," said Granddad.

"You have captured us well, and I'm that pleased you've added yourself into the picture. My! My! You have such a talent, Patrick. I will keep this forever." And so he did.

After leaving Granddad's house, Patrick and his mum happily strolled home together occasionally stopping to speak to people they knew along the way.

As they got closer to home, Patrick felt a little awkward but asked his mum about the new baby. Sarah ruffled his hair just like Granddad always did.

"Well," she said, "your little brother or sister should be here before the end of July."

Patrick grinned and asked if he could think of some names for the baby.

"Of course, you can. But I rule out the name Tarzan."

She knew that Patrick loved the Tarzan stories. They were both still laughing about the name Tarzan, as they walked into their house. Unfortunately, they didn't realise Simon was back home.

"Can't a man get any peace on a Sunday afternoon, without you two being so bloody loud?"

He scowled at them both. "And it's about time you came home, Sarah!" Before she could make any reply, he reached out and slapped Patrick across his face then told him to get out of his sight! Frightened, and not understanding why his father had hit him, he ran up to his bedroom. Sarah was so angry she was growing to hate this husband of hers.

"Why did you do that? What on earth is wrong with you these days? He's just a child and didn't deserve to be hit like that!"

She was shaking with her anger and felt so sorry for Patrick. Simon didn't say anything, but pushed past her and left the house, slamming the door behind him. She quickly went up to Patrick's room to see how he was.

Patrick was sitting on his bed looking so very sad. She took him into her arms and said how sorry she was.

"Oh, Patrick! I never thought your father would hit you like that. Please forgive me!" He looked up at his mum and gave her a watery smile, his big brown eyes full of tears.

He looked down at the floor and thought about telling his mum how often his father had hit him before, but he kept quiet; he didn't want to worry her or his granddad. She then led him into the bathroom, where she put a cold flannel on his sore face to soothe it. Both went back down into the kitchen, where Sarah made him his favourite Ovaltine drink.

They both sat in silence for a while. Sarah was anxiously watching him whilst he drank the Ovaltine. Patrick drank all he could to please his mum and then asked if she didn't mind him going back up to his bedroom. He said he wanted to read a book he was enjoying. But really, he just wanted to be on his own.

She followed him up the stairs, and gently looked at his sore face again, before leaving him sitting on his bed. She went into their living room, and almost fell into the armchair; she couldn't contain herself any longer and softly wept. After slamming out of the house, Simon hadn't realised, but he had walked all the way to Wolverton. He had nearly walked all the way to where he worked. Still preoccupied, he turned onto a towpath that led down to the great river Ouse. He leaned against a tree trunk and just stared at the river, he felt inside his trouser pockets for his cigarettes and matches. Blast! His pockets were empty, apart from a handkerchief; he was angry all over again and was desperate for his cigarettes.

Although deep down he knew he shouldn't take his temper out on Patrick. He just couldn't seem to stop his outbursts; he knew his temper was getting worse. Even at work, he was quick to be angry, especially with his employees. But as far as he was concerned, he was the manager, for goodness sake, and his staff needed to be aware of that. He managed an accounting office, with ten staff, as well as his secretary, and expected high productivity, from each, and every one of them. His standards were high at work. In his arrogance, he expected his employees to look up to him, especially as he had come through the war and was a sergeant. He insisted his staff addressed him as Sergeant Smithers; it made him feel even more in command.

Eventually, he turned away from the river and walked slowly back home. All was quiet as he entered the house; both Sarah and Parick had gone to bed.

Chapter 2

July 1948

The new baby had arrived! Patrick was at home as it was the school holidays. Earlier that morning after his father had left for work, Patrick's mum asked him to fetch Mary from next door. He was aware that the baby was on its way, and almost flew next door to get Mary.

"Please come quickly, Mary, I think my mum needs you."

Mary patted Patrick on his head and told him not to worry, but to also fetch Mrs Cooke, the midwife.

Off he went at lightning speed to find Mrs Cooke. He was so thankful after knocking on her door that she was at home. Picking up her medical bag, she followed Patrick back home. He then waited in the kitchen for what seemed a very long time, not daring to go out.

Eventually, Mary came into the kitchen and made a pot of tea. "It won't be very much longer now, Patrick," she said, "but Mrs Cooke and I are that thirsty."

After just a few more hours, which seemed a very long time to Patrick, he heard the baby crying. Mary who had a big smile on her face appeared in the kitchen again and told Patrick he had a little baby brother.

He was so pleased and smiled back at Mary, asking if his mum was alright.

"Your mum is tired, but just fine," she said, as she patted him on the shoulder.

"Now, I'm going to the telephone box to ring where your father works. I expect he would want to know the news!"

Mary kept things close to her chest, but she didn't like Sergeant Simon Smithers one bit; he could be a difficult man.

On many occasions, Simon had made it clear, that he didn't like Mary very much either. But Sarah had asked Mary to try and get the baby news to him.

So, off she went to the nearby telephone box. Patrick went along with her. As soon as Simon heard about the birth, he left his office, leaving a supervisor in charge and swiftly walked home. After the call was made to his father, Patrick collected his bike from home and rode over to his granddad's house to tell him the baby had arrived. Thomas was so pleased to hear about the baby's arrival, and his lovely Sarah was well. He wanted to visit her that very minute.

However, Patrick told him about Mary calling his father at his office, and that he was on his way home. So, Thomas decided it would be best to wait and see Sarah and the baby the next day instead. When Simon had received the phone call at his office, he hadn't thought to ask if it was a boy or a girl. But he was very pleased to discover it was a boy. They had decided to call the new baby Matthew.

Simon thought the baby looked just like Patrick did when he was firstborn. This concerned him; he didn't want another Parick, and he wanted a son to be proud of. And a son more like himself; he saw himself as strong without any weaknesses. He didn't like weakness in anyone. He was still very critical of Patrick's quiet ways and irritated that he preferred to read books and draw. Simon would not admit it, but he was also deeply jealous of the closeness that Patrick had with Sarah, and his granddad, and was determined to enrol him into the army cadets as soon as he was old enough, whether he wanted to or not!

October 1948

Baby Matthew was now just over three months old. Sarah felt happy with her daily routine, although during the night was a different matter. When Patrick came home from school, he always played with Matthew, so that his mum could get on with making their evening meal. He was being as diplomatic as an 11-year-old could be, especially knowing his father's routine, and how annoyed he would be if his evening meal wasn't ready by 6 pm on the dot.

Patrick was holding Matthew on his lap, pulling funny faces at him. "Oh! Look, Mum! He's laughing at me."

Sarah turned away from the sink, where she was preparing the vegetables, and sure enough, little Matthew was chuckling. "Well, I never! That's his first chuckle!"

Patrick felt very proud of that. It warmed Sarah's heart to watch her two sons together.

"What's for dinner tonight, Mum?"

"It's sausages and mash," she called, "along with cabbage, and afterwards, we have a jam tart."

Patrick pulled a face at the thought of cabbage, Sarah laughed at him. "Just a small piece of cabbage for you, Patrick."

Later, they ate in silence, which was something else his father insisted on. Luckily, little Mattew had fallen asleep inside his pram. After their meal, Patrick's father went into the living room to read his newspaper. Patrick looked at his mum and asked if he could go up to his bedroom. He was very keen to use his new easel.

She ruffled his hair just like Granddad did, and said, "Off you go." He didn't hesitate and ran upstairs to his bedroom, taking the stairs two at a time.

Later that same night, their sleep was disturbed again by the baby. Sarah picked him up out of his cot and took him into the living room, where she hoped he wouldn't disturb Simon. She fed him and changed his nappy, but still, little Matthew wouldn't be pacified. Simon banged on the bedroom floor with his fist. He was angry at being disturbed by the baby yet again.

He threw back the bedcovers, stomped into the living room, and shouted at Sarah, "Can't you keep him quiet just for once?"

"Stop shouting, will you? You can't expect a baby to stop crying by shouting at him, you're just making him worse and frightening him."

"Well, get him to shut up, will you? You're his mother, for God's sake! You should know why he bloody well cries half the night."

The next morning after getting Patrick off to school, Sarah settled Matthew into his pram; he looked so cosy wrapped up against the chilly October morning. She set off for the baby clinic, wanting to ask their advice to settle Matthew's tummy. She suspected he had developed some colic.

The district nurse at the clinic was helpful and recommended some gripe water. "I'm sure that will help," she said. Sarah thanked her and pushed the pram back outside. Just as she stepped down onto the pavement, two women were walking by. "Oh, it's Sarah."

She looked up, and there stood Jane and Pamela; they all smiled as they greeted each other. All three had been at school together. "We heard you had a new baby boy."

Still smiling, they both looked inside Matthew's pram.

"Goodness! He's the spitting image of Patrick, isn't he?" Sarah smiled, agreeing he was indeed the image of his big brother. She told them we had named him Matthew. They both agreed that was a lovely name and chatted for a while longer, each asking after each other's families and promising to meet up again very soon, with all three deciding to meet in their local café, later that week. Sarah was already looking forward to that. As Matthew was looking so contented inside his pram, she decided to walk a little further and visit her dad. Thomas was so pleased to see them and ushered them inside.

"Well, this is a lovely surprise," he said. He went into the kitchen to put the kettle on for a cup of tea. At the same time, he reached inside the kitchen cupboards for Sarah's favourite ginger biscuits. They both sat down at the kitchen table with their cups of tea and biscuits. Sarah told him all about her morning, and how lovely it was to have bumped into Pamela and Jane. And, about her visit to the clinic as she suspected Mattew may have some colic. As she was talking, she looked over to the pram where Matthew was sleeping.

What she didn't realise was the troubled look on her face. Thomas noticed though, but waited patiently for her to tell him what the problem was. He made conversation and asked how Patrick was getting on at school.

Although he knew that Patrick was doing well as he visited his granddad as often as he could, and loved to tell him all about his school, especially his favourite lessons and his friend Robert. Sarah didn't like to worry her dad but needed to confide in someone she could trust, and she valued his thoughts.

"It's Simon, Dad. I know that being a sergeant in the war must have been dreadful, and settling back into civilian life isn't easy for him. Also, I knew before we married that he was a complicated man, but I loved him very much, and he loved me, we wanted so much to be together."

She looked down at her hands in her lap. "I guess, it's the war that's changed things. He finds Matthew crying at night difficult to cope with, which has made him irritable and difficult with all three of us."

Thomas listened carefully to his daughter and was worried, as he didn't have the answers to give. Just lately, he had found Simon to be even more difficult than usual and had never really got on very well with him, although he tried very hard to do so.

You would never guess that Thomas felt that way; he was always very friendly and polite towards his son-in-law, Thomas looked at his daughter who he loved so much, and knew it had taken a lot for her to confide in him like this. He cupped his chin in his hand and thought of what to say.

Eventually, Thomas patted Sarah's hand and said, "Would it help if I had a little chat with him, you know man to man, that sort of thing? Perhaps he is finding civilian life harder than he thought it would be and finds it difficult to talk about how he feels. I should think there are lots of men and women just like him, right across the country struggling to regain their identity after so long. I tell you what! He goes to the George for a beer or two on Sunday mornings, doesn't he? So, I will turn up there as well. Maybe after a pint or two, he will mellow a little, and we can talk things through. Don't worry, Sarah, I won't mention the conversation we've had."

Sarah wasn't ever so sure about her dad's idea but trusted him to know what to say. Little did they know, Thomas wouldn't get the chance to have that conversation with Simon. Sarah had just washed up the dishes after their evening meal and decided she would finish off the curtains she was making, especially as Matthew was taking a nap. The curtains were for the local café. Sarah thought what a coincidence it was, as she was going to meet Jane and Pamela there for a cup of tea, hopefully later on in the week. The curtain material was a lovely buttercup yellow, the sort of colour to make you smile thought Sarah. She knew they would look very pretty in the café windows, and thought about mentioning some matching tablecloths, that would look really grand.

She was thinking of how to mention the tablecloths' when she was disturbed by someone banging very loudly on their front door. She was beaten to the door by Simon closely followed by Patrick. Simon threw the door open, and there stood Percy Pearce, the butcher.

Sarah instantly knew something was wrong. Percy usually had a big smile on his face, which he didn't have this evening. Simon couldn't help to show his annoyance. "What the hell are you banging on my door like that for?"

Percy ignored him, looking at Sarah, he said, "Can you come quickly? It's your dad. I think he's had an accident."

He quickly explained how he had found Thomas.

"I went to your dad's house for our usual game of chess and found him lying on the floor at the bottom of the stairs. I've left your dad's neighbour Dora with him, and the doctor is on his way. But thought it best to come for you, Sarah." Her face drained of colour, she snatched her coat from the hall stand and followed Percy out to his van, calling over her shoulder as she went, for Patrick to look after the baby, until she got back. Patrick was also visibly upset and wanted to go with his mum to see how his granddad was.

Instead, he walked through the house, and into the kitchen to check on the baby as his mum had asked him to. As he looked inside the pram, little Matthew let out a loud cry and didn't seem to want to stop. Patrick rocked the pram gently like he often watched his mum do, and spoke softly to Matthew trying to settle him.

Patrick didn't notice at first until his father spoke. He turned to see his father leaning against the kitchen doorway.

"Well, just look at you! Quite the little mummy, aren't you?"

Patrick ignored him and continued to rock the pram, even though Matthew's crying seemed to be getting louder. Simon walked over to the pram and pushed Patrick out of the way. "Here give him to me, I will see to him."

He pushed Patrick to one side, and picked Matthew up from his pram, carrying him into the living room. Matthew was still crying very loudly, Patrick was worried and followed his father.

"What are you following me for? Do you still want to play a mummy or something?"

He could see his father was becoming very agitated, and even more worried when Simon held baby Matthew high up in the air; he was shouting at the baby to stop crying.

"Please, don't do that, Father, you're frightening him, and you may hurt him. He's just a baby!"

Patrick reached out to take the baby from his father. Simon pushed him away, his hands somehow slipping, and little Matthew fell to the floor. The baby lay there very pale and still. "Now look, what you have done, you've killed him!"

Patrick was frantic; he bent down to pick his little brother up. "Don't you dare touch him, you've killed him."

"No, I haven't."

"You shouldn't have held him up high like that. You've made him cry even more and frightened him." Patrick looked down at his little brother again and said he was going to run and fetch the doctor.

Before Patrick could do anything, his father shouted, "You had better run and hide, boy. You've killed your baby brother! No one would believe I would harm him. I'm the war hero around here, and don't you forget that! Not one person would believe you, boy. I'm respected around here for my military background, and I will make sure to tell everyone, you were jealous of your little brother, and threw him on the floor, in a jealous rage."

Patrick was overwhelmed with shock; how could his own father do this to him, and say such terrible things?

He looked down at baby Matthew again and wanted to cry. "Now get out of my sight! Just get out of here, and don't come back, and don't think you can run to your precious granddad either. Because he's dead!"

Simon's face was contorted in spite, he told Patrick, "Whilst you were playing at being a mummy, Percy Pearce came back, and said your granddad had a heart attack, and he's gone to that big place in the sky."

Patrick looked around frantically thinking of what to do; he ran from the house; he didn't want to be anywhere near his father. He ran feeling disbelief in what had just happened. He ran and ran, without knowing where he was running to, all the time thinking of his baby brother, and what his father had said and done. He was so shocked that his father could do such a terrible thing.

Patrick was numb with grief when he thought of both his granddad and baby brother. And his mum.

Oh! How would his mum feel, when she was told he had killed his little brother? She would never forgive him.

On and on Patrick ran, until he felt exhausted and slowed down. He was plodding now, just about putting one foot in front of the other. Still feeling the disbelief of what had happened, his heart was breaking for his little brother and granddad. Sarah quickly climbed out of Percy's van and running inside her dad's house, she was greeted by Dora who was kneeling by his side.

Dora looked up at Sarah, smiling she said, "He's going to be alright, my love. I think he may have fainted, but he's looking better now; the colour is coming back into his face."

"Oh, Dad! Have you hurt yourself anywhere?"

Thomas reached out and patted her hand, saying, "I think I've hurt my ankle."

"Percy has asked the doctor to come, so just lay still until he arrives."

Just then Dr Drake arrived, "Hello, Thomas, let's have a look at you then."

After examining Thomas, Dr Drake said he had sprained his ankle, and he couldn't see any other damage. With the support of Percy and the doctor, Thomas was carefully lowered down onto his sofa. The doctor strapped up his swollen ankle, resting it on a cushion for comfort; Sarah covered her dad with a blanket to keep him warm, and made him a cup of strong sweet tea.

She stayed with him for another hour, before deciding she had better go home, in case the baby needed her.
Percy offered to drive her back home again. Dora, kindly said she would stay with Thomas for a while longer.

Sarah could hear the baby crying before she even walked through her front door. Simon was stomping around the room, with the baby on his shoulder. She reached up taking the baby from him, talking to the baby softly whilst rocking him gently in her arms.

As she was soothing him, his crying turned to hiccup. She thought he looked very pale and could feel a lump on the back of his head, which wasn't there before.

Looking up at Simon, she asked, "What happened, he isn't usually this upset, and I can feel a lump on his head."

Simon shrugged saying, "How would I know? Patrick was looking after him when I went out."

He could see the confusion on her face, adding, "I wasn't gone for long."

"You mean you put your children before the pub? Patrick shouldn't have been left alone with a baby to look after."

He smirked at her, saying, "I thought he liked playing at being a mummy."

Sarah was shocked at his nastiness towards his own son, and to leave a baby for the pub!

"And where is Patrick?"

"I sent him to bed. he said he had a headache."

Sarah was carrying Matthew as she climbed the stairs to Patrick's bedroom; Simon followed her, blocking her way into Patrick's room.

"He's asleep. What's the point of disturbing him?" He said. Sarah was to regret her next movements, instead of going closer to Patrick's bed, she just peered around his bedroom door. She didn't want to disturb him.

Sarah woke the next morning to the sound of baby Matthew softly crying in his cot. She lifted him out and fed him whilst she was still in bed, and noticed there were some bruises around the lump on the back of his head.

Concerned, she went down into the kitchen to speak to Simon about it again. But he wasn't there, *very strange*, she thought, *he usually wants a cooked breakfast before work.*

From the bottom of the stairs, she called to Patrick, "It's breakfast time!"

There was no answer.

Goodness, she thought *he is a sleepy head this morning*, which wasn't like Patrick at all. She dashed into his bedroom, pulling back the covers, there were pillows placed inside the bed where Patrick should have been. Feeling sick with panic, she ran from room to room, shouting for Patrick. Then she ran back into his bedroom, looking under his bed and inside the wardrobe. She went back downstairs again, still calling out for Patrick. Feeling very panicked now, she searched everywhere, before going out into the garden, looking inside the garden shed. His bike was still there, just as he left it.

She went next door to ask Mary if she had seen him, but she hadn't. Mary also looked concerned; she knew Patrick wasn't the sort of boy to worry his mum like this.

Sarah desperately looked everywhere again, still calling out Patrick's name. Then she thought, maybe he had woken up early and gone to see his granddad. But then why would he put his pillows inside his bed like that, it didn't make sense. With her heart pounding, she put Matthew in his pram, and almost ran with him, through the streets to her dad's house. Her dad, was just how she had let him the previous evening; he was still lying on the sofa, with his ankle resting on a cushion.

She said, "Is Patrick here, Dad?"

"No, lass, I haven't seen him. I expect he will come to see me after school later though."

"He's missing, Dad. His bed hasn't been slept in and I can't find him anywhere. I thought he may have come to see you before school; he was so worried about you last night, although he wouldn't have come here without telling me."

Thomas's face went white. He tried to get up off of the sofa. Sarah pushed him back down. "Stay there, Dad, I'm going to the phone box to ring the police, And Simon."

Tears were raining down her face as she left to make the phone call. Thomas put his head in his hands. "How can he go missing like this? It just isn't like Patrick."

Percy arrived to see how his friend Thomas was, just as Sarah had left. Thomas told him, "They couldn't find Patrick." Percy looked very concerned.

It wasn't long before Sarah returned; she was pleased to see Percy sitting beside her dad, as this was a dreadful shock for him. She quickly explained, "I must go back home, Dad, the police are coming to my house, and Simon is on his way home from work."

Percy said he would stay with Thomas for a while longer, so she hurried home, pushing Matthew into his pram as fast as she could. A policeman and a woman arrived; they quietly listened to what Sarah told them, making their notes at the same time. It was difficult for Sarah to get her words out; she was crying like her heart would break.

Simon who had arrived home, kept very quiet. He didn't add anything to the conversation, answering their questions with a yes or a no. "Firstly," the policeman said, "we will speak to Robert, Patrick's friend, and of course, we will be paying a visit to his school."

The officers left, saying they would be back soon. The police headed towards Patrick's school, wanting to speak to both his teacher and the headmaster, who both confirmed that Patrick wasn't the sort of boy to cause any worry, not to anyone!

Both agreed he was an excellent pupil and said there was no cause for concern regarding his schoolwork either. Whilst the police were at the school, they also spoke to Robert; he told them that Patrick always called for him to walk to school together. But that morning, he didn't arrive, so Robert just thought he was ill, and walked to school without him, he was worried to hear Patrick couldn't be found.

The police asked Robert if he and Patrick had any favourite places where they liked to play. Robert said they did and gave the police a few places to look. The police visited Sarah and Simon again, explaining they had spoken to his teacher and headmaster, and Patrick's friend Robert, telling them Robert had given them a list of where they both liked to play.

So firstly, they would be looking in those areas, and of course, speaking to the neighbours. The police also wanted to look inside Patrik's bedroom, and did Sarah have a photo of him they could have. Sarah looked across at the framed photo of Patrick, which was sitting on top of their cabinet; he was wearing his school uniform and smiling into the camera. Tears were running down Sarah's face as she gave them his photo.

Mary from next door had noticed the police car outside Sarah's house. Going around to see if she could be of any help, she also told the police that this wasn't like Patrick at all. At that moment, Sarah's dad arrived. He was helped into the house by Percy.

"I couldn't wait at home any longer, Sarah. Has there been any news of Patrick yet?"

Sarah shook her head and cried her heart out. Thomas took her in his arms and cried with her. Simon was looking very uncomfortable, which didn't go unnoticed by the police. A search for Patrick soon started, with the police knocking on people's doors and asking questions.

They also visited the places where both Patrick and Robert played.

Later that day, the police returned to Sarah and Simon's house to tell them there was nothing to report just yet, but they would keep searching. Later, Percy returned to their house to take Thomas home in his van. Thomas felt he shouldn't leave Sarah, but she was aware her dad needed to rest, especially after his fall and his ankle was still swollen.

She promised him that he would be contacted as soon as there was any news of Patrick. As soon as her dad and Percy had left the house, "It was you! Wasn't it? Something happened here last night, when I went to see my dad. And you knew Patrick wasn't in his bedroom, didn't you? You deliberately stopped me from looking into his bedroom, didn't you? Well, didn't you?"

Simon looked away from her and wouldn't answer, "Answer me," she shouted. "You stopped me from going into his room and deliberately placed the pillows, so I thought he was asleep. How could you do that to your own child and what happened to Matthew, how did he become bruised like that?"

Still, Simon wouldn't answer. She was so upset, pummelling his chest in anger; he gripped her wrists tightly and pushed her away. Turning away from her, he promptly left the house; she heard the door slam behind him. Wrapping her arms around herself, she fell to her knees on the floor and sobbed. Hearing Matthew cry, she wiped her tears picking him up; she rested her cheek, next to his soft baby skin, taking comfort from his closeness. Looking up at his mum, he smiled and gurgled at the same time. Again, she buried herself in his softness and his baby smell, just holding him in her arms. That night, she slept fitfully waking up several times, just thinking of Patrick. She felt numb inside and so very helpless. She got out of bed long before it was light, still thinking of Patrick, the grief was overwhelming her. She looked inside Matthew's cot, expecting him to still be sleeping, but there he was smiling up at her, so like Patrick, it broke her heart. Sarah picked up the baby from his cot and walked into Patrick's bedroom, hoping in stupid hope that it was all a bad dream. His bed was empty! His favourite Tarzan book was still lying open at where he had got to.

The easel his granddad had lovingly made for his birthday, stood there in the corner. She removed Patrick's favourite jumper from his wardrobe, and held it to her face, after a while she hung it back up. With tears pouring down her face again. She left his bedroom, making her way back down the stairs again, where she fed the baby and settled him down. There was no sign of Simon, she thought that was good! She didn't want to face him today. Hearing someone knock at the front door, she ran to answer it, thinking it might be the police with some news.

It was her dad and Percy, Percy had kindly driven Thomas to her house again. With both Sarah and Percy helping him, Thomas hobbled inside. He took Sarah into his arms as best he could; they both broke down and cried again.

Percy watched with great sadness, after a while, he left them saying he would call back later to take Thomas home again.

Her dad asked her if the police had been back with any news of Patrick; she shook her head sadly. Thomas tenderly held his daughter, stroking her hair whilst she cried again. Through tearful eyes Sarah, looked at her dad, telling him what she had found out.

"It's Simon, Dad. It's because of him that Patrick is missing." She told her dad how Simon had prevented her from looking inside Patrick's bedroom that night. "Simon told me, Patrick was upset over you, and had gone to bed with a headache, so I shouldn't disturb him. All I did was peep around his bedroom door, and there he was lying under his blankets; at least, that is was what I thought."

She started to cry again. "If only I had looked more closely! Simon had placed pillows inside his bed, so I would think he was asleep."

Thomas was shocked to the core. "Why on earth would he do that?" He could hardly believe the man could be so cruel to his own son. "So, Patrick could have been missing for longer we realised?" Sarah nodded her head.

She went on to tell him, of the baby having a lump on the back of his head, and about the bruise that came out the next day. Thomas took Sarah's hands into his own. "We must tell the police all of this as soon as possible."

She looked distraught and left the house to call the police from the phone box. The policeman at the other end of the phone call, listened carefully to what Sarah said, whilst making his notes. He kindly told her to go home and wait for the police to arrive. He said they would be there almost immediately. It was the same two PCs who came the last time.

PC Pete Bishop and PC Kate Stewart sat down and waited for Sarah to speak, she was finding it difficult. She said that Patrick went missing the night her dad fell and sprained his ankle. She told them of Simon's behaviour preventing her from going into Patrick's bedroom, and how his pillows were placed. She put her head in her hands and cried again, finding it difficult to continue.

Thomas finished for her and told the police about the lump Sarah had found on the back of the baby's head, along with the bruises that appeared. Both the PCs looked at each other. They had been suspicious of Patrick's father when they first met him; their instincts were correct.

They asked Sarah where her husband was. She replied in a dull voice, "I don't know."

Chapter 3

After the argument Simon had with Sarah, he hadn't gone very far; in fact, he was sitting on their garden bench, at the bottom of the garden. He was staring at the houses beyond their garden, watching a man digging in his vegetable patch and a woman in another house cleaning her windows. Simon was staring without really seeing anything, his heart was heavy inside his chest. He ran his hands through his hair, and thought *why the hell, did I let my temper get the better of me again?*

Taking out his cigarettes, he smoked the whole packet without realising. He knew he shouldn't take his aggression out on Patrick, but God help him, he couldn't seem to help it. Getting up from the bench, he walked back towards their house. He didn't go inside; instead, he just stood there, looking up at the house. He thought back to when he and Sarah had first got married they were so very happy. He walked back to the bench; sitting down again, he started to think back to when they first got married.

They had a church wedding, It was a blissful sunny day. He was wearing his army uniform. Sarah looked beautiful in her white gown, they had met at a dance just a year before. Simon loved her so much that he gave up his army career to spend as much time with her as he could. He had just a few more months to serve before taking up a position in an accounting office. Simon couldn't remember his parents; they both died when he was very young. He couldn't even remember what they looked like. After they died, he was sent to live with his father's sister; his aunt Mavis in Bradwell. Aunt Mavis had never married, preferring it that way, as she didn't particularly like children.

However, she loved cats, who she showered with love and attention. Wherever Simon looked, there always seemed to be a cat curled up somewhere. Aunt Mavis had so many cats that Simon had lost count of them all. She didn't talk very much to Simon; he often wondered if she cared at all.

His clothes were always clean and ready for school, and a meal was ready for him in the evenings, but she didn't speak to him a great deal; he became a lonely child. As soon as Simon became old enough, he joined the army. He loved the army life, and completely focused on his future there; he worked hard and eventually became a sergeant.

Until the day he met Sarah when everything changed. One weekend, whilst on army leave, Simon and three other soldiers heard of a dance to be held somewhere near Wolverton. It took some persuading to get Simon to join them, he hadn't been to a dance before and didn't know his left foot from his right foot, where dancing was concerned. However, he eventually agreed to join the other three, setting off to find the dance hall.

As they marched into the hall, all four drew lots of admiring glances. They looked so very smart in their uniforms; the buttons on their tunics sparkled under the lights, and their boots shone like mirrors. Together, they ordered beers from the bar, whilst looking around for a spare table to sit down. On the stage at the far end of the room, a band was paying. As Simon looked around, he could see lots of people tapping their toes to the rhythm. A few couples were dancing around the dance floor.

Whilst the soldiers were enjoying their beers, they were also looking around the room at the pretty girls. Two of the soldiers left their table to ask someone to dance, leaving behind Simon and his friend Micky. Across the room, Simon could see a group of girls all chatting to each other, and tapping their toes to the music. One of the girls caught his eye; he thought she looked beautiful, with her fair skin and soft blonde hair, which seemed to shimmer as she moved.

Micky could see where Simon's attention was drawn to, and indeed she was a very pretty girl. Looking at Simon, he said, "What are you waiting for?"

Simon wasn't sure and hesitated especially as he couldn't dance. Micky spurred him on, by saying, "Well, if you don't ask her, I will."

Simon glanced across at her again; her eyes met his. She smiled, which gave him some courage. Standing up, he walked over to her. He introduced himself and asked if she wouldn't mind dancing with him. Smiling, she looked up at him, replying, she would love to.

The pair of them made a handsome couple as they moved around the dance floor. He bent forward and asked her name. Sarah, she said. From that moment on, Simon was smitten! He could hardly take his eyes off her. Sarah was equally enchanted by the tall handsome soldier. He apologised to her for his awkward dance moves, telling her he was a terrible dancer.

She replied, saying, she wasn't that good herself. They had two more dances together, before deciding to sit down. Simon was keen to get to know her; he looked around the room for an empty table, preferably in a quiet corner, his solder friend's soon forgotten. He wanted to be with Sarah, they talked quite easily with each other. Simon told her a little about the army. She, in turn, told him about her job in the haberdashery, and how she lived in Stony Stratford with her dad.

Before they knew it, the dance hall was beginning to empty, people were going home. Sarah looked around for her friends; they were going to catch the last bus home together. She spotted Jane and Pamela standing by the door waiting for her. At the same time, Micky tapped Simon on his shoulder, "Time to be heading back, old mate!" Crestfallen, Simon didn't want to part from Sarah. He turned to her asking when he could see her again.

She said she would like that, so they agreed on a time and a place for the following Sunday. Simon continued to reminisce, by thinking about their wedding day, and their honeymoon in Weymouth. Travelling by train, they arrived there very excited to be together forever at last. They were to stay in a guest house, which overlooked the beach below.

They duly arrived at the guesthouse, where they were greeted by a Mrs Butler, who Simon quickly named an old battle-axe! At the same time as greeting them, she promptly gave them a list of things they would not be allowed to do, whilst under her roof!

She gestured for them to follow her into what she called the honeymoon suite which turned out to be a tired-looking room, with a thread-bare carpet, and the window frame rattled in the sea breeze. Sarah rushed over to look out through the window. "Oh look, Simon! We have a wonderful view of the sea."

Simon embraced her from behind, resting his chin on top of her blonde head; she leaned back into him, whilst they both admired the view. He gently turned her to face him and kissed her passionately. Sarah happily unpacked their suitcases, saying, "Let's go for a walk, it looks so pretty out there."

"Not as pretty as my bride," he said. When they eventually left their room, Mrs Butler, the battle-axe, was waiting at the bottom of the stairs for them. She had her arms crossed across her ample chest, wearing a grubby apron and asked where they were going.

"Just for a walk," replied Sarah.

The battle-axe told them, "Well, don't forget the front door is locked at 10 pm sharp. So, if you're not back by then, you will be locked out."

With that, she shuffled away in her shabby slippers, back into her own quarters. Sarah and Simon could hardly contain their laughter and were still laughing at the battle-axe as they walked towards the seafront, where they were soon strolling along, with their arms wrapped around each other, looking very much like young lovers.

They found a bench to sit down, on and were quite happy to just sit, holding hands and admiring the view. It was very pretty, with the sun glinting on the sea. After a while, they decided to stroll a little further, stopping to watch two children, who along with their parents, were fishing for crabs. The children proudly showed them, the crabs they had already caught.

Both Sarah and Simon looked inside their bucket; resting at the bottom were two crabs, looking back at them, with their beady black eyes. Arm in arm, they continued with their stroll before coming to a group of children sitting on the sand, watching a Punch and Judy show. The children looked mesmerised by the antics of the puppets. They watched for a while enjoying the show, which finished with lots of clapping and laughter.

Simon asked Sarah if she was hungry.

"Now that you mention it, yes, I am."

"Come on then, let's go and get some of those lovely fish and chips I can smell."

Soon, they were settled down again, looking out at the sea, whilst eating their fish and chips. "They were the best," said Sarah.

They made sure to return to the guesthouse long before 10 pm. Sarah suddenly felt a little shy; it was their first night together as man and wife. But she needn't have worried, Simon was aware of how she felt. He was kind and gentle in expressing his love for her. The next morning, at breakfast time, they both got the giggles again. The battle-axe shuffled into the breakfast room with a pot of weak tea, and two mugs that she slammed down onto the table. This was followed by a bottle of milk; it wasn't even in a jug!

"I suppose you want sugar," she said. They both nodded, not daring to look at each other, in case their giggles escaped again. She shuffled backwards and forwards from the breakfast room firstly, with their sugar, shortly followed by two plates, each with a greasy fried egg, one piece of bacon, and one sausage; at the edge of the plate, she had slopped some tomatoes. They both tried their best to eat it before pushing their plates away.

The battle-axe shuffled back into the breakfast room to clear their plates away, looking down at them with disgust as they had hardly eaten anything.

Simon said, "Thank you, but for the rest of the week, just toast would be fine." Then both of them dashed from the room quickly, before bursting into fits of giggles again.

"That was ghastly," said Sarah.

The rest of their honeymoon was wonderful, just being with Sarah was all that Simon wanted. So long as he had her, he would be happy. Their time in Weymouth went by in a haze of love, happiness and intimacy, but all too soon, it was time to return home.

Home to them was with Sarah's dad Thomas. He kindly welcomed them to stay, until they could afford a home of their own. It was a while before the two of them could even think of looking for a house. They both saved every penny they could, until at long last, they did have a small deposit and started to look at houses for sale. Sarah wanted to stay in Stony Stratford if they could. She didn't want to move too far away from her dad.

Together, they looked at four houses, before deciding which they liked the best. It was a house on Church Street. As soon as they entered the house, they both knew this was the one for them. Sarah worked in a haberdashery shop; she loved her job there, amongst the lovely fabrics and accessories. She enjoyed helping her customers, to choose dress patterns, along with a suitable fabric. And could just imagine the lovely curtains she could make for their new home.

Before the moving day arrived, Simon received a letter from a solicitor. He had never received such an official-looking letter before, and just looked at it.

"Oh, come on, open it," said Sarah, whilst she and her dad were looking on. Simon opened the envelope slowly, almost frightened of what may be inside. As he was reading through the letter, the smile on his face was getting bigger and bigger. Turning to Sarah, he picked her up. Swinging her around the room, he put her down again, saying, "You won't believe it, you just won't. We, my darling wife, have just been given five thousand pounds."

Sarah and Thomas looked at each other in disbelief. It wasn't until they all read the letter again, twice over, before it sank in.

Simon told them, "My aunt Mavis died a while ago, leaving her nest egg to me. She had no other living relatives." He had told Sarah and Thomas some time ago, how he had been brought up by his aunt Mavis. Simon was abruptly brought back to the present.

He was still sitting on the garden bench when two shadows fell across him. He looked up; standing in front of him were PC Bishop and PC Stewart.

"Will you step back into the house now, Sergeant Smithers? There are questions to be answered."

He followed them back inside. Sarah was still sitting on the sofa with her dad; her eyes were red and swollen from crying. Both of the police officers sat down, but Simon didn't; he remained standing. He was thinking to himself, *may God forgive me, but I can't tell the complete truth. Sarah would never forgive me.*

PC Bishop led the questions. Looking at Simon, he said, "What can you tell us about the time Patrick went missing?"

Again, Simon ran his hands through his hair. "Well," he began, "the baby started to cry, just as Sarah left the house. Patrick lifted him out of his pram, but he seemed more upset than usual. So, I took him off of Patrick, and put him over my shoulder, to help soothe him, but he cried even more. Patrick reached up to take him from me. But somehow between us, the baby fell onto the floor, he banged his head, and was stunned for a while; he was lying very still; it was quite frightening. I'm sorry to say, I shouted at Patrick. I felt it was his fault; that he was responsible. If he hadn't reached up and taken the baby, he wouldn't have fallen like he did."

"I shouldn't have shouted. I'm sorry. He became very upset and wanted to fetch a doctor, but I could see there was no need for that. As he was so upset, I sent him up to his room, and that was the last time I saw him." Simon didn't dare tell them about the pillows, or of how cruel he had been to Patrick.

PC Bishop went on to mention how Sarah had found Patrick's pillows. Simon denied knowing anything about that. Both the PCs thought that there was more to this than Sergeant Smithers was prepared to say.

PC Bishop continued, "We have been informed, and believe it is out of character for your son to have run away. So, thinking about that, could you have intimidated Patrick so much, that he did, indeed run away from home?"

Simon felt ashamed; he dared not look towards Sarah. He was aware she was crying again. He just shook his head.

Chapter 4

Further down the road what was known as Watling Street, Bill and Alan were looking forward to getting home. Bill was driving their small lorry, at the same time as he was talking to Alan, his partner in crime. They always referred to each other as partners in crime; they both found it to be funny. Contrary to that, they were both skilled carpenters and had just undertaken a job in Towcester. The pair of them had been building a new stable block, at Towcester racecourse; it had taken them longer than they thought it would. So, they were both very keen to get back home to Woburn but still had a fair few miles to go just yet, and they still hadn't reached Bletchley!

"Shall we stop for a hot drink in Bletchley, Bill?" Alan asked. Bill wasn't so keen he just wanted to push on and get home. He needed a good night's sleep, in his own bed beside his wife Doreen. They had been working in Towcester for four days, and to save their hard-earned money, they had both slept in the back of their lorry. They thought it was a good idea, instead of staying in a bed and breakfast place which would cost a bit. Mind you, it wasn't the most comfortable of sleeps; they were both nursing back ache and were very tired.

It had become very dark whilst they were driving along, and was raining hard now. The lorry's headlights picked up a shape walking by the side of the road. "Can you see anything by the road, Alan? I thought I saw something then."

Bill slowed down, and they both peered out into the darkness. "Flipping heck, Bill, it's a child out there."

Bill pulled over to the side of the road, bringing the lorry to a stop. They continued to look through the rain, and sure enough, it was a young boy they could see. He was walking very slowly and was soaked through by the rain.

Alan said, "I think we should ask him if he's alright; he could be lost or something." Alan grabbed his coat and climbed down from the lorry.

"Hello," he said, "can we help you, are you lost?"

Patrick didn't acknowledge Alan; he just carried on walking step by step. Alan walked along with him getting very wet himself.

"My name is Alan, and my mate is called Bill. We are just driving home, and we're concerned to see a young boy like yourself walking alone along the road, and it's beginning to get very dark. Can we help you in any way?"

Again, Alan asked him if he was lost. Patrick still didn't answer; he seemed unaware of Alan, his head was down against the rain, and he was soaked through, but just kept on walking. Alan looked back at the lorry and gestured with his hands to Bill, "What do we do?" He climbed back inside the lorry.

"That boy looks very troubled, Bill, and he didn't even seem to realise I was trying to talk to him." Both men were thinking of what to do for the best.

Bill said, "We're not far from Bletchley now. How about we stop there and make a call to the local police station, and give them the boy's whereabouts?"

They both agreed that was about all they could do but felt worried for the boy as they drove on towards Bletchley.

As Bill and Alan drove into Bletchley, they looked out for a phone box. They soon found one on a street corner and called the local police station. The phone was answered by Sergeant Phillip Fletcher; he listened to what they had to say and took down a few notes. He tried to sound interested but he wasn't. He was coming to the end of his five-day shift and didn't want any distractions.

He'd arranged to meet his brother in London and was very much looking forward to a few evenings out with him, Maybe a restaurant or two, and perhaps they would even see a show. He shouted down the corridor for police officer Jack Taylor. Jack hurried to the front desk. "I'm here, Sergeant, is there a problem?"

Sergeant Fletcher looked down his nose at Jack; he didn't like him. He was always too obliging and eager to please. Fletcher resented him as he showed qualities of being a good policeman, which made him jealous. Unfortunately, Sergeant Fletcher wasn't a very nice person at all.

"Right! It's been reported there's a boy walking alone along the A5, he's walking towards Bletchley about two miles away. So, I want you to drive out that way and see what can be done, maybe he's lost or something."

PC Jack Taylor looked concerned and said, "Right, Sergeant, leave it to me." He collected his coat and the car keys and set off.

Jack was pleased to be driving the police car; it was a Wolseley. He had only driven it once before, and could hardly wait to get behind the wheel again. He drove cautiously at first as it was a dark and wet night, but then he accelerated enjoying the feel of the car. He wished he could take the car home to show his mum and dad; they would be so proud of him, although they were already very proud of their son, especially as he had become a police officer.

Jack was enjoying himself. He had almost forgotten what he had been sent to look for, which made him feel ashamed of himself. Giving himself a good talking to, he got on with the job. Slowly, he drove along the road for a while longer, eventually seeing what looked like a person walking along the road. Like Bill and Alan before him, he drove past Patrick and then stopped just in front of him.

"Hello," he said, "my name is PC Jack Taylor, and why are you walking along the A5 on such a wet and dark night, and on your own?"

Patrick didn't stop; he continued to slowly walk straight past Jack. Jack very swiftly stepped in front of him and gently put his hand on his shoulder. With that Patrick paused, but he didn't look up.

"Now, that's better," said Jack, "just because I'm a policeman doesn't mean you're in any kind of trouble. But earlier tonight, some men reported to us at the police station, their worries about seeing a young boy walking alone along the road. It's a lonely road to be walking along in the dark, so can you tell me where you're heading?"

Still, Patrick didn't look up or speak. Jack was concerned. The boy looked so downcast and so very sad. He made the decision to take Patrick back with him to the police station so that they could establish what was going on here.

He gently guided Patrick towards the police car; Patrick did as he was told as if he was in a trance. He allowed Jack to help him into the car. Then Jack drove off back towards the police station. On their journey, he asked what his name was, but again he didn't respond, he just looked very distressed.

Jack knew something wasn't quite right here, and felt sad for the child, and hoped they could help him back at the station. When they arrived back at the police station, Jack carefully parked the car and walked with Patrick towards the police station door. He pushed the door open for him and guided him towards Sergeant Fletcher. Fletcher looked disinterested at Patrick but asked him his name and address.

Patrick didn't or couldn't answer; he kept his head down just looking at the floor. Sergeant Fletcher was annoyed that he wouldn't look up, or answer him. Jack explained he wasn't able to answer. "Sir, I think he's had some sort of trauma."

"Trauma! Where do you get these words from, Jack? Just put him in a cell for a while will you, perhaps that will bring him to his senses."

"But Sergeant, he's wet through, and doesn't look well at all."

"Are you disobeying me, PC Taylor?"

"No, sir! Of course, not! I'm just a bit concerned about him, that's all."

"We are police officers, not nursemaids, just put him in a cell and get on with it."

Jack led Patrick to a cell, gently sitting him down on the bed. He then rushed off to find a blanket, the boy was shivering. Gently, he put the blanket around his shoulders, then hurried off again to make him a cup of tea. He wasn't sure if the boy would like tea, but thought a warm drink was what he needed. Whilst Jack was playing nursemaid which was how Sergeant Fletcher saw it. Fletcher had an idea.

He quickly dialled his brother Reg's number; they exchanged a few words, before Sergeant Fletcher said, "I have a boy here, that you may be interested in."

He told him a few things about Patrick. "I would say he's around ten or eleven years old."

Reg was very interested. "Bring him with you tomorrow, Phillip. I do have a few vacant beds that need occupying. After all, I can claim more funding from my benefactors."

Their shift was coming to a close, and both Jack and Sergeant Fletcher were looking forward to a few days away from work. Before Jack left for home, he went into the cell that held Patrick and asked him once again if he was alright and if there was anyone he could contact for him. Patrick was still sitting on the bed with the blanket around him. He didn't respond to Jack's kindness. Jack sighed and left the boy sitting there.

Sergeant Fletcher told Jack to get off home. "But I have another twenty minutes of my shift to finish, Sergeant."

"I know you do, I'm not stupid! But it's quiet here, you may as well get off now."

Jack thanked the sergeant, informing him the report about the boy was still on his desk. Saying cheerio, he left the station and rode home on his bike.

Sergeant Fletcher walked down the corridor to Jack's desk, removing the report on the boy. He shoved the report inside his jacket and walked into the cell which housed Patrick; he pulled him to his feet, saying, "You're coming with me, boy!" Patrick didn't resist. Sergeant Fletcher took him outside and over to his own car. He unlocked the car door and pushed Patrick inside, telling him to sit still until he came back.

Sergeant Fletcher walked back inside the police station, just as Sergeant William Judge and PC Luke Davis arrived for the next shift.

Sergeant Judge asked, "If there was anything to report?"

Sergeant Fletcher said, "Nothing at all, Sergeant, it's been a very quiet night. In fact, it's been a very quiet few days."

He then calmly collected his coat and left the station. Sergeant Fletcher was feeling smug as he drove out of the station car park. It was a dull dark morning which helped conceal them both. When Fletcher arrived at his house, he got out of the car, opened his garage door, and drove his car inside, leaving Patrick still sitting there. He went inside his house, quickly changing out of his uniform into something more casual. He realised he still had the report about the boy inside his jacket, typed very neatly by PC Jack Taylor; with annoyance, he threw the report down on his dining table.

Going into his kitchen, he threw some cheese that looked past its best into a paper bag, along with some bread and an apple for the journey.

Picking up the suitcase he had previously packed, he promptly left the house.

Going back into his garage for Patrick, he very gruffly told Patrick to follow him. Fletcher walked very swiftly towards Bletchley train station; they didn't have to wait long for a train. Pushing Patrick onto the train, he pointed to a seat where he wanted him to sit, seating himself away from him, but also keeping him in his line of vision. For a while, Patrick was lulled to sleep by the movement of the train; his head lolling to one side. The train had covered some distance via various other stations, before finally arriving at the destination Fletcher was looking out for.

He left his seat and roughly shook Patrick's shoulder. He woke with a start, wondering where he was for a while. Fletcher indicated for him to follow him. Patrick stood up unsteadily; he was feeling so very tired, but did as he was told and followed Fletcher. They both stepped down from the train, onto the station platform. He walked behind Fletcher until they came to an escalator. Patrick had only ever been on one train journey in his whole life before, and had never seen an escalator; he wasn't sure of what to do and hesitated.

Fletcher noticed and cruelly hauled him onto the escalator beside him. "For God's sake," he said, "will you hurry up? We have another train to catch now."

The train they needed to catch was a tube train; it was just a short journey before they stepped out onto yet another platform. This time, there were just a few steps to climb, before finding themselves in another ticket station. Fletcher's brother Reg was waiting for him outside a café as arranged. Whenever Phillip Fletcher met his brother, it was always outside the same café. The two brothers greeted each other warmly, with Reg asking his brother how his journey had been. Reg looked down at Patrick but didn't make any comment. The two men swiftly left the train station, followed by a very anxious and tired Patrick. With both men occasionally looking behind them, making sure Patrick was following them. They walked along a busy road for about 20 minutes. Patrick could hardly put one foot in front of the other before they eventually turned into another road, which wasn't quite so busy, turning again, into a tree-lined avenue, with large houses on either side.

Not very far along the avenue, they came to a gated drive. It was a very long drive, edged with various trees, and shrubs. At the end of the drive stood a large imposing Victorian house. Reg led the way towards the front door; as he walked inside, he shouted for the matron.

A woman appeared from a side door, and greeted both men, with a nod of her head. Over the years, she had met Phillip Fletcher. Addressing Reg, she asked, "Is this the child you mentioned?" He replied with a nod of his head.

He then said, "As you are aware, matron, I have a few days owing to me which I intend to spend with my brother," he indicated to his brother Phillip.

With that, both brothers promptly turned away and walked back towards the door from which they had arrived. Phillip Fletcher followed his brother to the side of the large house as he had on many previous occasions. Reg had a small flat of his own with his own private front door. He was very proud of his flat. He had his own comfortable living area, along with a kitchen, bathroom and two bedrooms; his office being in the main house.

"Right," he said, "let's get the kettle on for a cup of tea, before we decide on which restaurant we will enjoy later his evening."

In the main house, the matron looked at Patrick and knew instinctively this boy wasn't like the other boys that stayed there. She could see he had been cared for, and his clothes were of good quality. Patrick stood in front of her with his head bowed down. She asked him his name, not getting any response. She looked at him again, feeling concerned for this particular child. The matron was a strict woman; she had to be with twelve boys in her care. But there was something about this child she thought.

"Come along, I will show you the dormitory." Patrick swayed on his feet which didn't go unnoticed. However, she guided him up a sweeping staircase, which led to a long hallway, which had various doors leading off of it. He followed her to the very last door, inside were four beds, each with a bedside cabinet.

"This will be your bed," she said, pointing to the bed closest to the door. She led him back out into the hall and pointed out two bathrooms.

"We have eleven boys here," she said, "with you, making twelve. I will show you where the dining room is for supper in a moment. But first, I will show you the schoolroom." There were twelve desks inside the room, with stools underneath them. On the wall was a blackboard, and on another wall, was a map of the world, along with various bookcases.

The teacher's desk and chair were positioned in front of a window. "This is where you will have lessons," she said. "They will be every day with Mr Thompson our teacher. You will be taught arithmetic, English and geography. We also have what we call a quiet room; this is where you can read. Or if you prefer, you can play a board game with the other boys."

Matron then led him back down the staircase, into the kitchen and dining room.

Chapter 5

And so began Patrick's time at the Waif and Strays Society. True to her word, the matron led Patrick into the kitchen. The kitchen maid and cook, who were mother and daughter, had returned home until supper time. As the kitchen staff was not on duty, the matron made Patrick a snack of buttered toast followed by a cup of warm milk. After he had eaten, he was taken back to the dormitory, and told to get some rest, until supper time, which would be at 5.30. He lay down on the bed and promptly fell asleep.

Matron had her office on the ground floor, next to Reg Fletcher's office. She wrote a few notes down about the latest boy in her care and decided she would speak to Reg about him when he returned, although she doubted Reg would be interested in her concerns about one particular child. Unlike the previous manager, Reg seemed only concerned about the financial side of things. Matron suspected he used his position for his own monetary gain, although she had no proof of that. It was just a feeling she had.

The matron's name was Maggie Pritchard; she had worked at the Waif and Strays since she was 30 years old; she was now 50. She ran the home with strict discipline, which was required with twelve boys from various walks of life. But she was, in fact, a fair and honest woman. Maggie came from a good background; she was well educated by her father, who himself was an educated man; he passed on his knowledge to his only daughter until he eventually became ill, with Maggie needed to care for him until his death. To this day, she still misses her father greatly.

Patrick had been at the waif and stray's home now for two months. At the very beginning, he found it difficult to adjust to his life there, but very slowly, he came to accept it, although he still hadn't spoken one word to anyone.

Matron and Mr Thompson, the teacher, were particularly concerned about Patrick's lack of speech, although he seemed to be an intelligent boy and was well-behaved. Mr Thompson suggested that he may have had some sort of traumatic experience before he came to the home. The other boys in Patrick's dormitory ridiculed him at first, calling him names. The name Stupid was top of their list. However, as the months went by, they came to accept him, for the way he was. The other boys hadn't come from a caring family like Patrick had. They lived on the streets using their wits to survive, sometimes not even having anywhere to sleep and they were always hungry. They were forced to steal food when an opportunity arose; some of them became orphans in the previous world war; they were a mixed bag!

Patrick rarely saw Reg Fletcher; all twelve boys had strict instructions not to go near his office, which they adhered to. They were aware Mr Fletcher could be very unpleasant at times, and he was known to dish out punishment for bad behaviour. The one boy who seemed to have the most punishment was William Dent. William, on many occasions, had stolen food from the kitchen. He would steal from the other boys if they had anything to steal that was. He also stole from the schoolroom, books, pieces of chalk; anything he could lay his hands on. Then he would nastily, hide the stolen goods underneath other boys' beds, resulting in punishment for something they hadn't done. He was a problem and a bully!

Patrick and the other boys were very wary of him and learnt to check under their bed night and day. Christmas arrived at the Waif and Strays. Parick tried hard not to think of Christmas at home. Just the thought of his mum was painful, and more than he could bear. He knew she would be thinking of him as well, but would she ever forgive him for what had happened to baby Matthew?

And his dear granddad, to think he was no longer alive was difficult and so very sad. When Patrick did think of his granddad, it was to imagine him pottering around in his beloved garden, and he hoped, he was doing just that, up in heaven.

As for his father, he had blocked him from his mind completely. Christmas day at the Waif and Strays Society, started off the same as most mornings. Except for attending the nearby church, they usually only went to church once a month. The boys stood in the hall, waiting for Reg and the matron to lead them through the front door. As usual, they walked in twos towards the church and took their seats at the back of the congregation. The boys listened to the vicar as he read out his sermon from the pulpit. Not really understanding everything he said, especially as most of them felt abandoned in life.

However, they did realise they were fortunate to be part of the Waif and Strays Society. Apart from William Dent, who was usually very surly, especially knowing how unpopular he was, he didn't appreciate the society at all!

When the time came to sing Christmas carols though, William couldn't help himself and sang like the angel he wasn't, which made the other boys titter in amusement. Some of the congregation turned to see where the tittering was coming from, which resulted in the matron giving the boys a disapproving stare.

Back at the house, the boys all filed into the dining area, where they were greeted with their Christmas lunch, all prepared and cooked by Mrs Martha Harris and her daughter Sally. Both Martha and Sally stood proudly by the dining table, waiting to see the looks on the boy's faces when they returned from church.

Indeed, the boys' eyes nearly popped out of their heads, such was the sight of their delicious meal. In the middle of the table was a turkey; it had been donated by one of the wealthy benefactors. Martha and Sally smiled, leaving them to their meals, returning to their own home, where Mrs Harris's husband was waiting for his Christmas meal.

Matron took her seat at the head of the table where she could keep a close watch on them all. She carved the turkey passing the plates around to the boys, smiling to herself, at how lovely and quiet it was, whilst they tucked into their meals, apart from the munching of food that is.

Later that day, the boys amused themselves in what was known as the quiet room. Some played snakes and ladders; others played ludo or a game of cards. Patrick chose to read.

A few weeks later in the new year, three of the boys complained of not feeling very well. Matron tucked them up in her sick room, so she could keep a close eye on them.

One of the boys was Patrick; the matron noticed he had developed a rash over his chest. She was concerned and thought it best to call the doctor. Doctor Brown duly arrived.

After examining the three boys, he confirmed it was an outbreak of measles. All he could do was advise the matron to keep the three boys isolated from the rest of them, which she had already done and to make sure they drank lots of fluids and had plenty of rest.

Over the next five days, all three boys kept the matron busy. She put a note under Reg's door asking him to help oversee the remaining boys. He was reluctant to do so, instead, asking the teacher Mr Thompson to step in. Dr Brown was mostly concerned for Patrick. He didn't seem to be recovering as quickly as he would have liked. He voiced his concerns to the matron. "The boy in the far bed, matron. He isn't recovering quite as quickly as the other boys. I might need to admit him into the hospital, and he's very quiet though he hasn't said a word to me."

Matron led the doctor out of the sick room, and out into the hall. "Unfortunately," she said, "he hasn't spoken to anyone. When he arrived here, doctor, I could see he was different to the other boys who found themselves here."

The doctor asked in what way, was he different.

"Well," she began, "he looked as if he had been looked after. He wasn't malnourished or dirty, and his hair was cut nicely; also his clothes were of good quality. He also looked very sad when he first arrived here. The sadness isn't quite so noticeable now, but he just doesn't speak. Mr Thompson, the teacher, and I, both agree he's a bright boy; he nods his head for yes and shakes his head for no. Anything else, he gestures with his hands. But not one word has he spoken."

The doctor looked concerned, saying he may have had some sort of traumatic experience before coming here.

"Mr Thompson and I thought just the same," she said, "the other boys referred to him as stupid at first but they seem to have accepted him now."

Dr Brown looked very thoughtful and then advised he would call back tomorrow. It was the last Sunday of the month, which was the matron's afternoon off.

She felt tired after the measles outbreak but was thankful it was contained to just three of the boys. After all, it could have been so much worse, and luckily, two of the boys were recovering well, although she was still very concerned for Patrick. She usually spent her afternoons away from the boys' home, in her own house. Although she liked her accommodation in the boys' home, she also had her own little house, just a short bus ride away.

She felt very blessed that her father had the foresight to purchase the little terraced house she grew up in, and loved to spend her time there when she could. Maggie let herself into her house; it felt very cold, so she kept her coat on.

As always, she looked inside every room, making sure all was well, before retrieving some polish and dusters from the kitchen, and giving everywhere a good old polish as she liked to call it.

As she looked out through her kitchen window, and into the garden beyond, she noticed her spring flowers had started to poke through the earth, which never ceased to cheer her. Her housework was interrupted by a knock on her door, and there stood her neighbour, Connie French; they had been friends since their school days. Maggie and Connie smiled at each other.

"When you've finished your cleaning, Maggie, come next door for a warm-up by my fire."

A little later, that's just what Maggie did. The two women chatted over a hot drink and a slice of Connie's fruit cake, because of the rationing though, it was more cake than fruit! Maggie told her of the measles outbreak, and how lucky they were that it was contained to just the three boys.

She didn't mention Patrick but hoped he would be a lot better in the coming days. Both women chatted all afternoon, enjoying having a bit of gossip about some of the other neighbours until Maggie noticed the time. "My goodness, look at the time! I had better get a move on, or I will miss my bus."

After three more days, Patrick seemed to be making progress. Doctor Brown was pleased. He didn't feel the need to refer him to the hospital after all, which he had been reluctant to do anyway. Due to his lack of speech, the hospital would probably traumatise him even more, he thought.

The doctor was also aware the matron was a kindly person and knew the boy was settled in her care. After careful consideration, he decided not to pursue the lack of speech, hoping the boy would improve in his own time. Reg Fletcher was sitting at his office desk, looking through the letters he had received that morning. One letter was very interesting to him; it was regarding child migration to Australia. He leaned back in his chair and thought about it, thinking maybe he could get rid of some of the more difficult boys in that way.

He looked inside his desk drawer for his set of keys. Walking over to the filing cabinet, he removed a list of the boys' names. *Well*, he thought, *William Dent would be the first boy for certain, also the stupid boy who wouldn't speak.*

He looked down his list to see who else he could be rid of. A boy called George Hunt caught his eye; he was Dent's sidekick; he could go as well and good riddance to all of them. Reg realised he would need a name for the stupid one, the one who wouldn't speak. He thought for a while, then decided on the name of Alfie Grey. He knew of a chap called Alfie Grey, who he didn't like; in fact, he detested him.

The original Alfie Grey was the son of a wealthy benefactor, George Grey. Alfie Grey quite often attended the benefactor's meetings with his dad. At the last meeting, Alfie had enquired about the financial side of the Waif and Strays home. Reg managed to bluff his way through the questions, reassuring his benefactor that their financial help was greatly appreciated.

And all the funds were held securely in a bank account, he promptly took out a bank statement for them to see.

That seemed to shut up Alfie Grey he thought, until the next meeting.

But Reg was clever; he had been siphoning money donated to the home for many years, depositing it, into his own bank accounts. He had four other accounts in various different banks, using fake names and addresses. He was very careful though, and only transferred small amounts of money at a time; his little nest egg was building up nicely. He even had a stash of cash hidden in his flat next door, which he added to whenever he had the chance.

At the weekend, he always counted the money, along with a cigar and a glass of good whisky; he was in his element! It made him feel very smug to know he was getting away with it, what they don't know, won't hurt them he thought. He kept his money a secret from his brother, not because he was a copper, but because he knew Phil would want to be in on it. And there was no way Reg wanted to share with anyone, even his brother. Although his brother Phil was in the police, Reg knew he was as devious as he was.

Oh no! He thought. *It's best to keep all my money to myself, and one of these days, I will disappear, and live somewhere sunny and without a care in the world.*

His thoughts shifted towards later that night; he had planned to meet his lady friend Sally. She had got word to him that her husband was away for a few days. He couldn't wait. Before that though, he decided to reply to the migration office. He had written, saying he had three boys who would be very interested in a better life in Australia.

Reg knew to keep it hidden from the matron though, and Mr Thompson, knowing they wouldn't agree with him. He doubted they would see it as an opportunity for the boys, as stated in the letter.

Sitting back in his chair, he poured himself a large whisky and hoped he would receive a reply very soon. He was looking forward to getting rid of William Dent; the boy was a damn nuisance. Reg heard back from the child migration programme, a lot sooner than he thought he would.

The reply contained various forms to be completed for each child. He eagerly completed the forms that very day and returned them first class. Within two weeks, he received confirmation, that all three boys had been accepted, and a date was given for their journey. And so, it was arranged.

William Dent, George Hunt and Alfie Grey were to leave the Waif and Strays for Tilbury Port on 29 April 1949. The ship would be sailing at 5 pm that day. Reg was delighted the ship wasn't sailing until the afternoon; that gave him plenty of time to get the boys there.

He even had the foresight to purchase suitcases for each boy, and labelled them with their names. He had added one change of clothes in each case, along with a towel, toothbrushes, toothpaste and soap. All he needed to do now was borrow a car for the short journey to the train station. He had a friend he knew who wouldn't mind lending his car, especially if he bought him a few beers down at the pub. And tonight, that's where he intended to be!

29 April duly arrived. Reg was aware that after overseeing the boys' breakfast, the matron spent time in the kitchen, to discuss ordering various groceries with the cook. And the boys would now be in the classroom, to start their lessons with Mr Thompson. He saw this as his opportunity to secretly get the boys away. Reg marched into the classroom, startling both Mr Thompson and the boys.

He informed Mr Thompson, that three of the boys had dentist appointments that very morning, which he would be taking them to.

"Right!" He said, "I want, William Dent, George Hunt and him, pointing to Patrick." The three boys were startled and rather wary. Apart from handing out discipline, Reg Fletcher didn't usually take a lot of notice of them.

Mr Thompson said, "This is rather irregular, Mr Fletcher, the boys have only just begun their lessons."

Reg ignored him, telling the boys to follow him. Each boy got up from where they were sitting and followed Reg from the room.

Looking at them, he shouted, "Well, don't just stand there looking at me, get your coats and hurry up!"

Once they had their coats on, they did as they were told, and followed Reg out to the car, which Reg had cunningly parked outside earlier that morning. Unbeknownst to the boys or anyone else, he had previously stowed their suitcases inside the boot of the car. Reg only needed to drive for about ten minutes, before arriving at the train station. He parked the car, telling the boys to hurry, as they had a train to catch.

They were confused and anxious something wasn't quite right. Both William and George were streetwise and knew the lay of the land; you didn't need a train to visit the dentist, they instinctively knew Reg was up to something. Reg purchased their tickets, urging the boys towards the train platform where the train was waiting. The three boys sat anxiously on the train with Reg sitting beside them. No one spoke; they were feeling very tense and anxious, which was unusual for William Dent; he was proud of his streetwise reputation.

Eventually, the train came to a halt. Reg stood up and gestured for them to pick up their suitcases and follow him. With their suitcases banging against their legs, all three hurried along behind Reg.

They walked for quite a long way, before turning through a large opening; above the opening, it read Port of Tilbury. The boys looked at Reg for some sort of explanation; he just smirked and walked towards the ticket office. He produced the necessary paperwork for the boys to board the ship. They followed him again, finding themselves looking up at an enormous ship. He walked them towards the ship's gangplank, all three looked up at the ship, and they felt frightened and couldn't understand what was happening.

Reg stepped forward, explaining to them, they would be sailing to a country called Australia. All three looked at him in shock; they were scared stiff of the unknown, and reluctant to step onto the gangplank. But just at the same time, around thirty other bewildered young boys arrived to board the ship too.

William, George and Patrick were roughly pushed along with them and soon found themselves on the ship's deck. All three looked down onto the port below; in the distance, they could see Reg walking away. The boys were told to stand in a particular area on the ship's deck, where they were met by a stern-looking woman. She told them she was Miss Butler; their names were ticked off of a register along with other boys.

"Right, follow me!"

They all followed her down many flights of stairs, each with its own landing. It was getting more and more gloomy; she called over her shoulder for them to remember their way.

"I've told you to remember because if any of you forget your way, you will be punished."

The boys looked at each other with concern on their faces; they were already confused in the gloom, They continued to follow her along a corridor, where she suddenly stopped outside a door. "This is to be your cabin," she said.

The boys walked inside; there were six bunk beds lined up against the wall; there wasn't a port hole, and it was very gloomy inside. She barked at them to put their suitcases down. "Right! Follow me again. I will show you all where the washroom and toilets are, followed by the canteen, then the schoolroom. Just remember not to get lost, if any of you are found where they shouldn't be, it is punishment for you!" She rested her hand on a cane that was tucked inside a belt at her side.

The boys were all tired and bewildered, also very hungry, but no food came their way, not even a drink. Each boy had chosen which bunk they preferred, and promptly sat down, still feeling weary and apprehensive for their futures.

Just as they were having a rest, they heard the engines start to whirl, and the ship started to move. They were on their way to Australia! A land that some of them hadn't even heard of.

Patrick felt like crying; he was thinking of his mum. He thought he would probably never see her again; his heart ached. Two weeks of the journey had passed by; they were told it would be another two weeks or more before the end of their journey.

Patrick's and the other boys' day started with breakfast in the canteen. It was usually just bread with a smidgen of jam and a cup of water; they washed and dried their own plates and cups, then walked along the gloomy corridor to the classroom.

Their lessons were taken by Mr Gordon; he was stern but a lot nicer than Miss Butler. Patrick tried his best in the lessons. But it was soon noticed that he didn't speak, which concerned Mr Gordon, although he encouraged him. Patrick didn't utter a word.

Some of the other boys made fun of Patrick, which didn't escape Mr Gordon's notice. He was aware that he had a few boys in his class with various problems. Luckily, for the boys, he was a fair man, even if he did appear stern.

Their lessons finished at 3 pm every day, with the evening meal being at 5 pm, which gave the boys two hours of free time. This was the best time of the day for them; they felt free of the gloom from below deck.

Although they were only allowed to stand in a certain area of the deck, all of them loved being out in the open. They were amazed by the expanse of the ocean and the huge waves which rocked the huge ship; all they could see around them was water, which seemed to merge with the sky. Patrick found it mesmerising. He thought of the easel his granddad had made for his birthday and wished he could capture the ocean by painting it. But that thought brought back memories of his dear granddad, which made him feel so sad all over again. He realised his twelfth birthday must have gone by, whilst he was on the ship, and how his granddad would love to celebrate that. That morning just as the boys were finishing their last lesson of the day, Mr Gordon said he wanted a word with them.

He stood up and walked around to the front of his desk, folded his arms and looked at them all with sadness, he had got to know the boys and was concerned for their future. "Tomorrow, the ship will be docking in Sydney, Australia; you will all be disembarking. So, your journey on this ship will come to an end."

The boys threw up their arms and cheered!

"Now quieten down and listen to me. There is something else I want to tell you all. You will be transported to an orphanage, in a place called Orange. So, when the ship docks tomorrow, you are to follow Miss Butler down the gangplank, where a bus will be waiting to take you."

All of the boys were beyond disappointment; they had hoped to be placed with families, but nothing had prepared them for an orphanage.

Looking miserable, and saying their goodbyes to Mr Gordon, all of them made their way up onto the top deck. All of the twelve boys felt utterly disappointed, and very wary of going to an orphanage. William Dent said he would run away and get a job; a few of the other boys said the same thing. Patrick felt the same as the other boys; he hung his head in despair.

Chapter 6

New South Wales, Australia
Stanley Smith had just spent an enjoyable weekend at his sister Cecily's place, along with her husband Jeff and family, and was on his way home to his property on the outskirts of Gilgandra.

He had stopped in Dubbo, which was halfway home; he needed to stock up on various provisions. Eventually, the back of his truck was almost full of what he needed; he was just about to drive off when he heard loud shouting. Stan looked towards where the shouting was coming from; in the distance, he could see a stationary bus, where some people were waving their arms in the air. There was quite a disturbance going on, also lots of shouting, quite a commotion was taking place. It looked like mayhem amongst the confusion.

He continued to watch in disbelief, noticing four boys running in different directions, and being chased by a man and women shouting their heads off. Stan soon realised it was the orphan bus. That saddened him. He didn't want to watch anymore and was about to drive away when he felt some movement from the back of his truck.

Getting out of his truck he was thinking, *that's all I need, a flat tyre.* He inspected each tyre carefully, and they all looked to be fine. Scratching his head, he noticed the cover on the back of the truck had been disturbed; he lifted the corner of the cover looking inside. Looking back at him was a terrified boy; his eyes were wide with fright. Stan secured the cover again, got into the cab and slowly drove away from the area. Stan drove quite some distance away; a fair few miles, in fact, before he pulled over in a remote spot. Switching off the engine, he walked to the back of his truck, looking inside again. A very frightened boy was still looking back at him.

Stan told him not to worry, explaining they had driven far away from the orphan bus, and were in a very remote spot, where no one would see him.

"Let's get you out of there, and into the cab, where you will be more comfortable. I have a flask of water that you can have too."

Stan helped Patrick into the front of his truck, where he poured some water into a cup for him. He watched as Patrick drank thirstily, then poured out a second cup, not only did he look frightened, but he also looked so very thin, thought Stan.

"My name is Stan. What's your name?"

"Of course, Patrick didn't answer, but he nodded his head and gave a small smile of gratitude for the water." Stan assumed the boy hadn't spoken, because he was frightened and wary of him. So, Stan chatted to him along the way, telling him about his property and orchards.

"It's a large property he said on the outskirts of a town called Gilgandra, It's a bit isolated, but a nice place. On the property, we have hundreds of almond trees. Have you ever seen an almond tree?" Again, Patrick didn't answer but he did smile a little bit. Stan continued his journey.

It was starting to get dark which pleased Stan; he didn't want the boy to be noticed while driving through Gilgandra. With the motion of the truck, Patrick fell asleep; Stan glanced at him, thinking, *poor kid. And what on earth have I got myself into?*

Eventually, Stan arrived home; he gently touched Patrick on his shoulder to wake him up, and Patrick woke with a start, frantically looking around wondering where he was.

A very tall man appeared by the truck; both men greeted each other warmly. Stan left Patrick sitting in the truck for a while longer, whilst speaking to the other man. He was explaining about Patrick. He followed Stan into his house. As it was dark he couldn't see a great deal. Stan continued to chat to him, hoping it would reassure him he was safe. He showed him into a small but comfortable-looking bedroom.

"This is where you can sleep," he said, "I can see you are very tired. Just take off your shoes and climb into bed. I will see you in the morning," and closed the door behind him.

Patrick did as he was told and was soon fast asleep again. Although Stan was also tired, he didn't go to bed straight away. Instead, he went outside and sat in his chair on the veranda. He was soon joined by Elijah who sat down next to him. Both men quite often sat outside and talked way into the night, mostly about their work but tonight, it was about the boy.

Elijah and his wife Blossom were aboriginal people, originally from the Gamilaraay tribe. However, they were both very settled working for Stan; they thought of him as a good man. Elijah worked alongside Stan on the property, and Blossom looked after them with her cooking, along with numerous other things. Stan told Elijah again of how he had found the boy in the back of his truck. Elijah knew Stan was a big-hearted and caring man, but was concerned about the consequences of helping the boy to escape.

Stan also thought the same; however, they lived in an isolated area, so he hoped the boy would go unnoticed. "And anyway, if anyone should ask about him, I will tell them he's my nephew, who had come to stay for a while."

Everyone who knew Stan also knew his sister had two boys and a daughter. So, they both decided, if any problems were to occur, the boy was to be known as his nephew.

Stan woke the next morning as he usually did at 5 am. He quietly looked around the bedroom door where the boy was sleeping; he was awake and looking back at him.

"Well, good morning, young man, did you sleep well?"

Again, Patrick didn't reply. Stan was beginning to think something may be wrong, or was he still frightened. Stan gestured for him to get up.

"Come on, I will show you where the toilet is, and the shower. In Australia, some people call the toilet the dunny. So that will be a word you may need to get used to."

Patrick followed Stan; he led him outside to the toilet and shower. Patrick was surprised to find it outside. Stan could see what he was thinking; He threw his head back and laughed, saying, "Welcome to Australia!" Patrick quite enjoyed his outdoor shower; it felt nice to be clean. He put his dusty clothes back on.

"Right," said Stan, "now, it's time for breakfast."

Again, Patrick followed Stan; they walked across the yard, to another house where Elijah and Blossom lived. Both of them stepped up onto the veranda, but before Stan could knock on their door, it was opened wide by Elijah and Blossom with warm smiles on their faces.

Stan did his best to introduce the boy to Blossom and Elijah. Elijah gestured for Patrick to sit down. Stan sat down in his usual chair. Blossom put a cup of milk in front of Patrick, followed by a large jug of coffee for everyone else.

She passed plates of food around to each of them. Patrick's eyes almost popped out of his head when he saw his plate; he had never in his life seen a breakfast like it. There was even a steak. He looked at everyone as if to say is that all for me? Stan nodded and told him, "We always start the day with a hearty breakfast." Whilst Patrick hungrily ate his food, the adults looked at each other, all thinking the same thing. *Goodness knows what this poor child has suffered.*

He looked so lost and wary, and so very thin. They all felt so sorry for him and wondered what on earth had happened to him.

Blossom turned away from the table so that Patrick couldn't see how sad she looked. She promised herself that she would look after this child, and to try and ease the problems he had obviously been through. When breakfast had finished, Blossom cleared away their plates, but couldn't help to notice the boys clothes; they were very dusty and dirty.

Blossom said she would wash Patrick's clothes for him that evening, and have them ready for him again the next day.

Stan stood up from the table and gestured for Patrick to do the same.

"Would you like to see around the property?" He asked. Patrick nodded and smiled. Patrick was about to follow Stan when he stopped and turned around smiling at both Blossom and Elijah; reaching out his hand, he shook both of their hands, thanking them for their kindness.

That was the undoing for Blossom; the tears flowed down her cheeks.

"I will show you all around the yard first, then we will drive over to the orchards."

Patrick noticed quite a few outbuildings which he hadn't done the night before, as it was so dark. He showed Patrick into the largest of the outbuildings. "This is what is known as the bunk house," he said. "It's used mostly at harvest time; it's for the farm workers. A place where they can sleep and cook their food. Most of them bring their wives and children with them," he said. "They are mostly aboriginal people, like Elijah and Blossom. Harvest time usually turns into a jolly old time with lots of merriment and laughter."

Stan then showed Patrick another outbuilding; this one was slightly smaller and was mostly used for farm equipment. There was yet another building of about the same size, Stan told Patrick this one was used for storing fertilisers. Patrick could see large sacks of fertiliser stacked up high inside. He continued to follow Stan as they walked past various smaller structures with Stan pointing them out to him. Stan turned to Patrick, and asked him, if he liked horses, Patrick nodded that he did.

"Keep following me then!"

And as they turned a corner, Patrick could see a paddock with two horses; one was a chestnut colour the other being white. Both Stan and Patrick leaned against the paddock fencing. It wasn't long before both horses ambled over to them.

Stan couldn't help but notice Patrick's face light up at the sight of the horses. "I can tell you like horses," he said, "and it looks like they like you too. Would you like to know their names?" Patrick nodded his head.

"Well! Look at the chestnut one," which Patrick did. "Can you see how her fetlock is white?" Patrick nodded. "Well, she's called Socks! And the white horse is called White Lightning."

Patrick leaned over the fence to stroke the horses. Stan showed him just where Socks liked to be stroked, which was on her neck, she moved to rest her head against Patrick.

Stan was amazed. "Well," he said, "she definitely likes you. White Lightning is sometimes temperamental, so go easy with her, but she just about tolerates a rub on her nose."

Patrick carefully reached out and stroked her nose. White lightning stood still for a little while before she wandered off across the paddock. It was clear to see that Patrick loved the horses. Stan led him back down to the yard to get his truck.

"It's becoming very hot, so instead of walking over to the almond orchards, we will drive instead." Together, they walked back into the yard. Stan was about to climb into the truck when he stopped and thought, *the boy should have a drink before we drive off; after all, he wasn't used to the Australian heat.*

And so, they sat in the shade of the veranda, both enjoying a cool drink. Stan watched Patrick whilst he was quenching his thirst, wondering how on earth he came to be on that orphan bus. There were so many questions Stan wanted to ask him But he didn't want to course him any more distress; it was obvious he had suffered in some way.

Instead, he patted Patrick on the shoulder, telling him how fortunate he felt that he chose his truck that day, also reassuring him that his home was secure with himself, Elijah and Blossom.

"You will always have a home here," he told him, "for as long as you want."

Patrick's eyes filled with tears; he responded by nodding his head and smiled warmly at Stan. Stan sighed and again looked thoughtfully at Patrick.

He asked, "Would you mind telling me your name though? You could write it down on a piece of paper. We all feel dreadful referring to you as the boy." Patrick nodded a yes. Stan went inside the house, and soon returned with some paper and a pencil, placing them next to him; he watched as he wrote down his name.

Looking at what he had written, Stan glanced at Patrick, saying what a fine name that was to have.

"Right! Now, let's go and take a look at the orchards."

Patrick was standing quietly at the edge of the orchards just taking it all in. He was amazed at the immense size of the orchards; as far as he could see, there was row upon row of almond trees, all standing to attention underneath a dazzling blue sky.

"Splendid, aren't they?" Stan said. "There are three hundred hectares out there with three different types of almonds. And in July, they all start to blossom, which is a fine sight. You will love it at harvest time. Although it's a hive of activity with the farm workers arriving, and wait until you see the tree shaker machine."

Stan pointed towards a wooden building in the distance, "Come on," he said, "I really will show you the machine right now."

As they got closer to the building, Patrick realised just how huge it was. Stan pushed open the double doors. Inside, stood the tree shaker. It was a machine like nothing Patrick had ever seen before, it was enormous. Stan explained how at harvest time, it would shake the almonds from the trees. Patrick couldn't wait to see the machine in action. After showing him the orchards, they both returned to Stan's house.

Stan told Patrick, "After breakfast tomorrow, I will leave you in Blossom's care, as I must drive into Dubbo. Will that be alright with you?" Patrick nodded and smiled he liked Blossom.

Patrick spent an enjoyable morning, helping Blossom bake her bread; he hadn't long finished his breakfast, but the lovely aroma made his mouth water. The aroma also reminded him of his, mum which made him feel so very sad.
He could just picture her at home, in their kitchen baking her bread, listening to the wireless at the same time.

Blossom noticed Patrick looking very downcast, so she guided him outside to the veranda, smiling at him; she gently placed a plate of her freshly baked bread into his hands. They both sat on the veranda for a while, enjoying the bread before going back inside.

Blossom had some other jobs for Patrick to help with, which would keep him occupied until Stan returned from Dubbo. Later in the afternoon, they heard Stan's truck arrive home; Patrick went out to greet him. As Stan stepped down from his truck, he was grinning from ear to ear. In his arms, he was holding a puppy. "This bundle of fur is for you!"

He gently handed the puppy to an astonished Patrick. Stan told him it was a Labrador retriever. Patrick was very surprised and pleased, He felt emotional at the same time, Stan patted him on the shoulder, saying, "Let's take her inside."

Patrick gently set the puppy down on the floor; she scurried around the room sniffing in all the corners. Stan said, "When I drove into Dubbo earlier today, my intention was to buy you some belongings. But then, I saw this little puppy, sitting in the pet shop window, I couldn't resist her."

Looking at Patrick's face, he knew he had done the right thing. Leaving Patrick with the puppy; he returned to his truck and retrieved the rest of his purchases. Going back inside, he showed Patrick the clothes he had bought for him, along with some books he thought he might like, pens, pencils and writing paper. A few things for the puppy. One item he showed him, was a pair of gaiters. "These are for your protection against any snakes, especially when you're in the orchards, or near the horses."

Patrick was only half listening though, all his attention was on the puppy. Later that evening, Patrick left the puppy in his bedroom, whilst they had supper at Elijah and Blossom's house. Sitting together around the table, everyone enjoyed a meal of roast lamb. It wasn't long before Stan told them both about the puppy.

Blossom looked across the table at Patrick; she smiled at him, telling him to bring the puppy into their house, so they could all see her. Patrick didn't need to be asked twice he dashed off to fetch her. He was soon back proudly carrying his puppy, placing her down on the floor. She playfully ran around Blossom's kitchen wagging her tail in excitement.

Both Elijah and Blossom could see the happiness on Patrick's face, thinking what a wonderful gift the puppy was. Stan was a kind-hearted man. Elijah asked Patrick if he had a name for her. Patrick pulled out a piece of paper from inside his trouser pocket, he had written down the name he had chosen for his puppy. He had written Beauty. Everyone agreed she was indeed a beauty.

It was the middle of July; the almond trees were in full blossom, just like Stan said they would be and looked beautiful. Patrick helped in the orchards during the mornings, with Beauty by his side. She was growing into a lovely companion for him, and with Stan's guidance, Patrick had trained her well. Stan and Elijah did the necessary work in the orchards, along with two farm workers. Patrick would walk amongst the trees, looking for any fallen twigs, which he would remove putting them inside a container.

Stan had explained that insects could hide under the twigs and were harmful to the almond trees, so it was important to remove them. As Patrick walked through the orchards, always closely followed by Beauty, he also checked the water pipes for any leaks. Stan had explained to him how the irrigation was a lifeline to the almond trees. At noon, it was time for a break.

It was only Patrick and Beauty who went back into the yard; the others sat in the shade of the orchards for a snack and a drink. Patrick walked back to the house with Beauty close by, after a drink and a bite to eat. He would settle down at the kitchen table for his lessons. Stan always made sure Patrick had some schoolwork to complete, which he prepared every evening for him. He told him it was important to try and keep up with schoolwork, as best as he could. He had various books about English literature and arithmetic even some geography.

Stan had written down various questions for Patrick to answer, and he would check them all later that evening, it was the best that Stan could do. It was nine months since Patrick had arrived in Australia and was almost Christmas time. Patrick had grown very tall and was more confident in himself now. He looked like a different boy.

Although everyone who knew about Patrick, they were still concerned about his lack of speech. Stan felt it was time to introduce his family in Bathurst to Patrick; maybe he needed other people around him his own age for a while.

So, it was agreed, Elijah along with the farm workers would take care of the orchards, whilst Stan and Patrick spent Christmas in Bathurst. They set off early in the morning for their journey, with Beauty sitting beside Patrick.

After nearly four hours of driving with one stop on the way, they pulled into Stan's sister's place. His sister Cecily, along with her husband Jeff came hurrying out of her house to greet them. She smiled down at Patrick, and stroked Beauty's head, saying, "Come inside, you must all be tired and thirsty," leading them into her kitchen, where her three children were already sitting around a large table.

All three jumped up at the sight of their Uncle Stan; they were all very fond of him, greeting him warmly, along with lots of chatter and laughter. Stan introduced Patrick to them, he shyly nodded his head in acknowledgement.

Smiling at Cecily's boys, Stan said, "These two rascals are Ronnie and James, they're twins like myself and Cecily."

He then gestured towards his niece, "And this delightful young lady is Alice." Again, Patrick nodded his head.

Before Patrick could sit down, Alice grabbed his hand and pulled him towards the back door.

"Come on," she said. "I want to show you, my horse."

She wouldn't take no for an answer and pulled him through the backdoor. Beauty bounded after them.

Alice still holding onto Patrick's hand ran across the paddock towards the stables. Stan was concerned at Alice's eagerness to show Patrick her horse, and knowing how shy Patrick could be, he chased after them.

Alice was running so fast that she fell over, taking Patrick with her. As they both stood up, they couldn't contain their laughter; Stan had just caught up with them and was both amazed and overjoyed to hear Patrick laugh.

Well, I never, he thought. At the stable block, Alice showed Patrick her horse. "She's called Midnight. Isn't she just the best horse you ever did see?"

Patrick nodded his head, that indeed she was a fine horse.

She asked Patrick if he could ride; he shook his head. "That's odd," she said, "because Uncle Stan has two horses on his property, maybe you need to ask him, Patrick."

She told Patrick in a very disapproving voice, "My two brothers are not interested in horses at all, which is very disappointing for my parents. The only thing they are interested in, are cars and more cars."

She took hold of Patrick's hand again and walked away from the stables. "I want to show you our chickens next."

Patrick noticed, there were a lot more chickens than his granddad used to have.

She explained, "The chickens were fenced inside snake-proof wire, but don't worry, Patrick, the snakes usually only appear early in the morning or at night time."

Patrick knew all about snakes as Stan had explained all about them. "I suppose we had better go back inside. Uncle Stan will wonder where we are," she said.

Patrick thought he could stay with Alice forever; she was such good company, However, they headed back towards the house, with Beauty still close by.

The next day was Christmas Eve. The house was a buzz of excitement. In the living room stood a very fetching Christmas tree with sparkling lights and lots of tinsel shimmering in the sunlight from the window. This was Patrick's first Christmas in Australia, his last one being at the Waif and Strays Children's Home.

It did seem strange to him to have Christmas in the sunshine, but nevertheless, he was as excited as everyone else, and so pleased that Stan had brought him to Bathurst.

During the morning, Patrick helped Alice muck out the stables; he had done that quite a few times before on Stan's property, so he knew what to do.

After breakfast, the whole family walked into the town, for a Christmas service at the church. Afterwards, they ambled down to the river, to show Patrick around a little bit. The boys Ronnie and James wanted to show Patrick the racetrack.

"See, I told you," said Alice, "all they think about are cars and racing."

Cecily said, "Perhaps, they could show Patrick another time, as they needed to head back home now."

For a moment, both Ronnie and James looked downhearted, but not for long. Between them, they decided they would show Patrick their car collection when they got home. Ronnie and James led Patrick into their bedroom, their bedroom walls were covered in posters of different types of cars. Both of them were talking excitedly at the same time, explaining the cars to Patrick.

There were car magazines piled up on every surface and in every corner of their room. Patrick had never seen a room quite like this. He noticed amongst the cars, a sketch pad and a pencil lying on the floor. He picked them up, and with the twins looking over his shoulder, he started to sketch a racing car.

Both the boys were very impressed and promptly added the drawing to their bedroom wall collection. All of them were so engrossed with the cars, and enjoying each other's company that they completely forgot the time.

Until Jeff called them, telling them it was time for supper. Later, after they had all eaten their meal, the twins turned to Stan asking him if he would play the piano. Stan said, "But it's nearly your bedtime."

They both groaned. "Oh, please Uncle Stan." He pretended to stretch out his hands and twiddle his fingers before lifting the lid of the piano.

Patrick was very surprised, to say the least. He didn't realise Stan could play a piano. Everyone gathered around as Stan played some country music. Cecily joined in, by sitting down next to Stan and playing the piano keys from the other end of the piano. Patrick thought it was all wonderful.

Christmas Day 1949

Everyone woke early the next morning and enjoyed a hearty breakfast before going to church again. Patrick particularly liked the church, with its pretty stained glass windows, he didn't yet realise he had an artist's eye for everything he saw. They listened to the sermon, and sang Christmas carols, before heading home again.

Once they were home, Cecily handed around a glass each of hot chocolate with cream added on the top, which was enjoyed by everyone, especially Patrick; it was something he hadn't tried before, but he thought it rather delicious.

The adults ushered the children out of the kitchen, whilst they started to prepare the Christmas lunch. Cecily told them they were having a turkey, with all the trimmings. As they all left the kitchen, closely followed by Beauty, she was never far away from Patrick if she could help it.

"I know," said Alice, "let's play snakes and ladders, with the board game taken out of the cupboard; they all sat down to play," with Beauty lying next to Patrick's legs.

It was good fun, although Patrick thought the twins may have cheated a little. After a few games, both Ronnie and James said they would rather play with their car collection, and went back up into their bedroom.

Alice asked Patrick if he could play chess. When he shook his head, she offered to show him. They sat for quite some time playing chess, or at least Patrick tried to play.

Before long, there was a shout from the kitchen, dinner was ready, and what a meal it was thought Patrick, everyone enjoyed it. They even had Christmas crackers, which brought heaps of laughter at the terrible jokes. They were all wearing silly Christmas hats, and having a merry old time, and for dessert, they had plumb pudding with cream.

After their meal, they all trouped into the living room to open their Christmas gifts. Patrick had noticed quite a few nicely wrapped gifts' sitting under the Christmas tree. Alice, Ronnie and James, all knelt by the Christmas tree, eagerly looking for the gifts with their names on. Patrick was surprised to be given a gift from Cecily and Jeff, it was a jigsaw puzzle; he shyly smiled his thanks.

Stan then lifted a gift from below the tree and gave it to Patrick. He opened it to find a Tarzan book inside, and it was Tarzan of the Apes. Patrick held the book to his chest and tried to push the memories of home and his mum to the back of his mind.

His mum had given him the exact same book, a year or so before. He looked up and realised that Stan, his sister Cecily, and Jeff were all watching him, but smiled as if they understood. Patrick looked towards Stan, nodding his thanks. Now it was Patrick's turn, before leaving Stan's house, he had painted a home-sweet-home picture for Cecily and Jeff. Before they could say thank you, Patrick gave Stan a gift. It was wrapped in brown paper, which was all that Patrick could find. It was a painting of Stan's orchard. Patrick had painted it whilst the sun was setting over the almond trees.

The colours were beautiful. He had captured the evening sky, using orange, yellow and red, and along with the almond trees glistening it was stunning. Patrick wrote down that Elijah had helped him, by finding an old frame to put the picture inside. Both Stan his sister and Jeff were stunned; the painting was splendid.

Stan stood up and put his arm around Patrick's shoulders to thank him. "The painting is just splendid Patrick, I will always treasure it; you are a very talented young man to paint something like this."

At that moment, Stan couldn't have felt prouder, and thank goodness, he had been saved him from the orphanage.

It was Boxing Day, and it was decided they would all have a picnic in the parkland down by the Macquarie River.

Both Stan and Jeff's vehicles were needed to drive everyone; all of the children were very excited, especially at the thought of a picnic. Once they were parked, everyone carried something towards a nice shady spot that Cecily had pointed out. The children carefully put out the picnic blankets for everyone to sit on.

Cecily had been very busy, and with Jeff's help, they had produced a lovely picnic of turkey sandwiches, sausages, cheese straws and Scotch eggs, not forgetting the homemade soda. Patrick had never seen such a lot of food at a picnic, probably due to the rationing at home he thought.

After everyone had eaten, the twins Ronnie and James wanted to see how far they could skim some stones into the river. All four stood at the water's edge, trying to be the first one to skim a stone the furthest.

Much to the twins' annoyance, it was Alice who skimmed the furthest; she was very pleased with herself. Jeff set up a game of cricket, calling them all back to play, it was decided that James would bat first; Ronnie was to bowl the ball, but every time Ronnie bowled, Beauty ran away with the ball; unfortunately, she thought it was her ball! The adults found it all hilarious.

Patrick chased after Beauty, but she was very reluctant to let the ball go. He managed to take the ball away from her a few times. But every time Ronnie bowled again, Beauty chased after it again. Stan found a stick and threw that instead, trying to get Beauty's attention, but she only wanted the ball. Alice suggested they play hide and seek instead. Patrick was nominated to hide his eyes first. Alice Ronnie and James all ran off to find a hiding place.

After a while, Patrick found James hiding behind a hedge along with Alice. But he couldn't find Ronnie anywhere until he walked back to where the picnic had been. He noticed a big bump underneath the picnic blanket, and there was Ronnie giggling his head off. They were all very tired when they arrived back home.

Stan and Patrick were heading home very early the next morning, which made Alice feel sad. She asked her Uncle Stan if they could all visit him in the next school holidays which would be Easter.

"I'm so sorry," said Stan, "but Easter is a very busy time with the almond harvest."

Alice said, "Of course, sorry, I had forgotten about the harvest."

Stan thought for a moment. "If it's alright with your mum and dad, how about the September school holidays?"

Cecily and Jeff said they might be able to arrange that, which brought smiles from everyone, except for Alice. She said, "But September is ages away!"

Cecily suggested in the meantime, Alice and Patrick could write to each other. Patrick smiled and nodded at that idea.

"Right!" said Cecily, "now that's all sorted out, it's time for bed."

As the children were all in bed, the adults settled down for a beer and a chat. Cecily wanted to discuss Patrick with Stan, saying how concerned she was at his lack of speech. Stan had already explained to Cecily. He would like to take Patrick to a speech therapist, but couldn't due to the situation.

"And it could have implications for me," he said, "as I helped him to escape the orphanage that day."

Stan said he guessed Patrick's age to be around 12 or 13. Cecily said she thought the same. So, as far as I'm aware, when he reaches 14, he would have left the orphanage and been placed in a foster home.

"So, for Patrick's sake, until he reaches 14, I'm determined to keep his identity away from any authorities."

Cecily was quiet for a while, but added, "Patrick might have some family looking for him, Stan."

Replying and saying, he was aware that could be the case, but for now, it was all about keeping him safe and happy.

"Perhaps when he's older, I could help him to trace any family he might have, but I still know very little of how he came to be on the orphan ship."

Stan, Patrick and Beauty were almost home. As their journey became more and more rural and with the evening approaching, they started to see kangaroos hopping along over the ground in front of them.

Patrick always found the kangaroos fascinating. Beauty wasn't so sure and barked at them as they hopped by. Suddenly, Stan's property appeared in front of them.

Beauty made them laugh; she was excited to be home, she was barking, and her tail was almost out of control with its wagging. Stan stopped the truck so that Patrick could open the gates to the property. Patrick thought the house looked very welcoming; he always admired how lovely Stan's house looked, especially at evening time, as the sun was setting. It was a very traditional-looking Australian house, with its wide veranda stretching the length of it.

Blossom and Elijah heard them approach and came out to greet them asking if they had a good journey and enjoyed Bathurst.

Patrick smiled at them both, whilst Stan said they had a lovely time. And he would tell them all about it tomorrow; they both felt weary after the long journey home. They stepped into the house closely followed by Beauty.

Blossom had thought to put some food in the fridge for them. Stan said he must thank her in the morning; she was always so thoughtful. After a bite to eat, they turned in for the night, with Beauty sleeping at the end of Patrick's bed as she usually did.

Over breakfast the next morning, Stan described their trip to Bathurst; both Elijah and Blossom said how lovely it all sounded. Further to that, both the men started to talk about their work on the property, discussing the work for the rest of the week. Patrick was going to do his usual work of removing any dead leaves and twigs from around the base of the almond trees, making sure to eradicate any diseases.

Then at midday, he would wander back to the house for his lessons that Stan had set out. Beauty would usually take a nap by his side. Today though, as they had only just returned from Bathurst, Stan hadn't found the time to set lessons out for him. He was thinking about his mum and granddad and found himself wanting to paint them as he remembered them, sitting in granddad's garden.

His granddad with his kindly wrinkled face, and his mum, with her lovely blue eyes just like granddad's. He sketched little Matthew too, with his chubby cheeks and dribble on his chin, just as he remembered them all.

When he had finished, he put the paintings in his bedroom, hidden away inside a drawer. Thinking about his family at home made him feel very sad, he wondered if he would ever see his mum again. Time had gone by; Patrick had celebrated his 13th birthday. The harvest had begun on Stan's property; it was all hands on deck!

Elijah and Blossom's extended families arrived all eager to work. Patrick was watching as Stan drove the tree shaker machine it was colossal. He was fascinated, as he watched the huge machine do its job of shaking the almond trees.

The almonds fell, landing on the ground sheets the workers had placed underneath the trees. As Stan moved from tree to tree, the farm workers made sure the almonds were spread out into a thin layer, so they could dry in the sunshine. Patrick watched for a long time and helped where he could, finding the whole process just wonderful, making his mind up to try and sketch it later. Elijah always looked forward to harvest time, it was hard work and long hours. But he looked forward to seeing his own people, they were very keen to work in the orchards and kinship was important to them all. They respected Stan as their boss, knowing he was a good man, and enjoyed his hospitality.

There would be lots of merriment in the bunkhouse, later on that night, that's for sure. The harvest took just over two weeks to complete; the weather had remained sunny which was a godsend. The almonds had been collected, and taken to a sheller facility, and so the cycle would begin again on Stan's property.

Elijah and Blossom had said goodbye to everyone, except for two workers who Stan asked to stay and work for him. Both Stan and Elijah were very aware they needed the extra help. Patrick had been writing to Alice as he promised, and their letters were busily going back and forth.

Alice had written about her horse Midnight and told Patrick all about her school and favourite lessons. She often mentioned her annoying car-mad brothers, and sometimes Cecily would add a little note as well.

He loved receiving her letters, and always wrote back the same day. This time, he wrote back very animated, about the recent harvest, telling her all about the tree shaker machine and how huge it was. He also mentioned now the harvest was finished until next year. So, Stan would have some spare time to teach him to ride Socks his horse.

He was looking forward to it, although on the other hand, he was a bit worried, riding a horse was something he had never done before. Patrick's riding lessons had begun; Stan helped him up onto the horse's back.

He told him to sit up straight but to also keep his back relaxed and to hold the reins in a relaxed way. Patrick placed his feet in the stirrups and off they went, led by Stan around the paddock. Patrick felt nervous. It looked a long way down to the ground should he fall off.

After about half an hour, Stan said that would be enough for his first lesson. Patrick didn't want to admit it, but he wasn't sure if he enjoyed it or not.

Stan patted Patrick on the shoulder, telling him he had done well for the first time. "Tomorrow, we will have another lesson, and by the end of the week, you should feel more confident." Patrick wasn't so sure at all.

Later that evening, as they were relaxing on the veranda, Patrick was reading his Tarzan book and Stan having a beer.

A man appeared on the property; he was riding a push bike, and he looked very hot and sweaty. Coming through the gates, he rested his bike up against the veranda, and looked towards Stan, asking if he was Mr Smith. Stan told Patrick to go inside and take Beauty with him.

He was concerned about who this person was. Stan asked what he wanted. The man introduced himself. "My name is Mr Hill, I'm the headmaster of the local school. It's been brought to my attention that you have a child here of school age but isn't currently in school."

Stan's mouth went dry. He glared at this person in front of him, but he knew he needed to be careful.

Stan stood up, folding his arms across his chest, "Yes," he said, "I am Mr Smith. And can I ask, who told you about a child not attending school?"

Mr Hill replied, "That isn't your concern."

Stan was angry now. "You," as he pointed at the headmaster, "have come onto my private property, and accused me of not sending a child to school. I'm entitled to know how you came by that information, don't you?"

Mr Hill started to feel nervous about Stan and wished he had stayed at home and ignored the gossip from the postmistress. She had come to his school, telling him about a boy called Patrick on this property who didn't go to school. He didn't even think to ask her, how she knew about the boy. Instead, he was arrogant enough, just to arrive at the property, and insist the child goes to his school. Stan was getting angrier by the minute, but he knew he had better mention Patrick just in case anything went further.

He told him, "Yes, there is a boy here; he's 14 and my nephew, so what of it?"

Mr Hill started to back off.

But Stan stepped in front of him in a threatening manner and insisted on where this drip of a teacher had got his information from. Mr Hill was feeling even more nervous now, he could hardly get his words out. He stuttered and explained that the postmistress had brought it to his attention. Just then, Elijah appeared and stood next to Stan. With that, the teacher climbed back on his bike, peddling away as fast as he could, although rather unsteadily. Stan was furious and planned on paying the postmistress a visit; he suspected she had been opening Patrick and Alice's letters to each other. How else would she have known?

Stan was annoyed with himself, he had heard rumours about that post-women before. As a result of that, he preferred to use the post office in Dubbo. To think she would stoop so low, as to read letters from children, the women had no morals. Patrick was in the house looking very worried; Stan assured him everything would be alright.

He wrote on a piece of paper that his age was just 13 not 14 and would they be able to find out. Stan again assured him they wouldn't be able to. Patrick then wrote down the date of his birthday, he hadn't told Stan before.

He wrote down 'my birthday is the 6th of April 1937'.

Stan smiled. "I guessed your age to be around 13 and I was right. And guess what? My birthday is in April too, it's the 16th."

Stan could see Patrick was still worried by the stupid teacher turning up like that. He was worried too but didn't want to show it. The last thing he wanted was to draw attention to Patrick. He was determined to pay the postmistress a visit; she shouldn't be allowed to get away with reading people's private letters, especially children's.

From now on, along with his own post, he would take Patrick's letters to the post office in Dubbo. In the meantime, to cheer a worried Patrick up, he planned to take him to an art shop. The last time he visited Dubbo, he noticed a new art shop had sprung up, he knew Patrick would love that. And later that day, whilst they were in that area, he planned to take him fishing by the Macquarie River.

When Stan told Patrick of his plans, his face brightened up, especially at the thought of an art shop. "We will go tomorrow afternoon," said Stan, "and by the time we have driven there and visited the art shop, it will be cool enough for a spot of fishing."

Patrick ran across to the cupboard for his writing pad. He wrote, 'Thank you, Stan,' adding, 'Although you are not old like my granddad, you are very kind just like him.'

So, thought Stan, *Cecily was correct. Patrick does have family somewhere.*

The next afternoon, they set off for their journey into Dubbo. Beauty was sitting at Patrick's side, looking out of the window for kangaroos. She started her usual barking when she saw the kangaroos speeding past. Patrick ruffled her fluffy ears and laughed.

It wasn't a long journey; about an hour's drive. When they arrived, Stan parked up, and they walked along the dusty road, towards where Stan had noticed the art shop.

As they stepped inside, Patrick felt like he was walking into something magical, he didn't know where to look first. He was amazed by the vibrant colours of the artwork, which had been arranged along the walls. And he could hear beautiful music playing in the background. On display, were various paintbrushes of all shapes and sizes along with different paints. There were oil paints and watercolours and some that Patrick didn't know.

In one corner, there were even sculptures and all you needed to make your own sculpture. Looking around in wonder, he could see piles of paper and cardboard, as well as other items to paint on. He was in his element, which was different to Stan; he was keeping a firm hold on Beauty, especially with all these precious things around them.

He told Patrick he had better take Beauty back outside, where he would wait for him. Stan found a shady spot to sit and wait with Beauty. He was feeling pleased with himself, for noticing the art shop and bringing Patrick here. It was well worth the journey, just to see the happiness on Patrick's face. Patrick emerged from the shop still smiling; he spotted Stan and Beauty and walked over to them.

Stan asked him if there was anything he wanted to buy from the shop?

Patrick just smiled. He was aware he didn't have any money to buy anything, but he had thoroughly enjoyed visiting the art shop. Stan stood up still holding onto Beauty, and with his other hand, he gave Patrick a bright red wallet.

"This is for you," he said, "now why don't you open it?"

Patrick looked inside the wallet to find a ten-shilling note. He looked up at Stan in surprise. Stan patted him on the shoulder as he always did, saying, "It's to thank you, for your help in the orchards, you worked hard, Patrick, and deserve it."

Patrick leaned forward and embraced Stan, nearly knocking him over.

Stan laughed, saying, "Right, off you go! And buy what you want from the shop."

Patrick didn't need telling twice, dashing back into the shop. Stan sat down again in the shade with Beauty by his side and waited for Patrick. It was another hour before Patrick emerged from the shop, with his arms full of painting paraphernalia. He sat down next to Stan to show him what he had bought; the smile on his face was well worth the 10 shillings thought Stan. They stored Patrick's painting things inside the truck, before heading off to a café.

Stan knew of a place that accepted dogs, so long as they behaved that was. They settled Beauty with a drink of water, before looking for a spare table. A waitress pointed to an empty table at the back of the café. They sat down and both ordered eggs and chips, along with a pot of tea for Stan and a glass of milk for Patrick.

Their meals were hot and delicious and were soon all eaten up. After leaving the café, they walked a little further down the main street, turning into an alleyway, which led to a fishing tackle shop.

Stan didn't need any fishing equipment, but he did need to buy some bait. Leaving the shop, he drove towards the Macquarie River.

Both of them settled down on the water's edge, with their fishing rods at the ready. Beauty was sitting by their side just watching. Patrick couldn't help, but remember, the last time he went fishing with his friend Robert. He wondered how Robert was, He couldn't remember a time when Robert wasn't in his life, and they were almost inseparable. Suddenly, Stan shouted and jumped up.

"I've caught something," he said, as he reeled his catch in, Patrick rushed to get the landing net. It was a Gudgeon.

"Well, I'll be blown," said Stan, "I was hoping to catch a trout."

Nevertheless, he placed the Gudgeon in the landing net and lowered his rod into the water again. Patrick was sitting very still, hoping to catch the trout that Stan wanted. But it was another 20 minutes before either of them caught anything else. Stan shouted again; this time he had caught a Golden Perch. Patrick was still waiting patiently before he also caught a Golden Perch. "I think the trouts are hiding," said Stan.

They sat in companionable silence for quite a while longer, catching another four fish between them, two more Perch and two Gudgeons. The sun was starting to drop in the sky. Stan thought it was time to pack everything away and head home. When they arrived home, both Stan and Patrick, carried their freshly caught fish over to Ellijah and Blossom's house. Blossom had promised to cook any fish they caught, for their supper the next evening.

The very next morning after breakfast, everyone except Stan went about their usual day. Stan needed to spend some time, going through his accounts. He lifted his accounting ledgers down from the shelf, spreading them out over the table, and with his head bent down, he set to work. It took him over two hours of checking his receipts invoices and bank statements until he was satisfied everything was in order. He was about the clear everything away.

When Blossom arrived at the door with their freshly washed laundry, thanking Blossom, he took the laundry from her. Going back inside, he returned his ledgers to their rightful places. He was whistling away. As he began to put his laundered clothes in his wardrobe, still whistling, he picked up Patrick's clothing, taking them into his bedroom, placing Patrick's things inside his chest of draws.

Just as he was closing the drawer, he thought he saw something sticking out from underneath his shirts. Looking closer, he could see it was a folder. Stan was tempted to look a little further; he hesitated for a while, before removing the folder. Inside were various paintings and sketches. There were lots of Beauty, even himself and Elijah whilst working in the orchards. There were sketches and drawings of Blossom, whilst she was baking bread in the kitchen. And a beautiful painting of Stan's house, nestled against the setting sun.

He was amazed by Patrick's talent, flopping down on Patrick's bed; he continued to admire his work. At the very bottom of the folder were paintings that really caught Stan's eye. There were three paintings, one was of an elderly man, sitting in what looked like his garden he was smiling. Stan wondered if that could be Patrick's granddad.

There was also a painting of a woman, who looked very pretty she was also smiling. Stan wondered who she could be; there was also a painting of a chubby baby. He carefully put everything back where he found it, and closed the drawer. Cecily, Jeff and the children were coming to stay soon. He would mention it to her; he wanted her thoughts on what he had found.

Chapter 7

It was September. Cecily, Jeff, Alice, Ronnie and James, all arrived for a week's stay at Stan's place. You would have thought they would be tired after their long journey. Instead, they all seemed full of energy, and excitement to be at Stan's. Blossom had been busy preparing the bunkhouse for them. It was decided Stan's two workers would stay in Elijah and Blossom's house, whilst his family were here. The family were to stay in the bunkhouse.

Beauty was running around like a dog with two tails; she was so excited with all the fuss she was getting. The twins, Ronnie and James, had some new cars to show Patrick and hoped he would paint them so that they could be added to their wall collection at home. Alice wanted to see the horses and was interested to know how Patrick's riding lessons were coming along. Patrick had to admit he wasn't doing very well.

Alice said, "Never mind, I will teach you!"

Like before, she grabbed Patrick by the hand and led him off towards the horse's paddock. As Patrick was with his art, so was Alice with horses; she was passionate about them.

She quickly saddled up Socks, looking at Patrick, and she said, "Show me what you can do."

Patrick gingerly mounted the horse, and very slowly walked Socks around the paddock.

"Gosh," said Alice, "you're such a novice." Patrick felt a little hurt by that. He just wasn't as confident as Alice. Alice realised she had been unkind to Patrick, and apologised.

"Sorry, Patrick, I've grown up with horses and have been riding forever. Let's play hide and seek instead; come on, we will ask Ronnie and James to play as well."

They left the paddock, wandering back into the yard, looking for the twins. However, walking towards them was Stan.

"I was just coming to fetch you two," he said, "we've decided on a picnic lunch and are almost ready to leave."

Using two vehicles, they set off for a nearby parkland. After eating their picnic lunch, they did indeed play hide and seek, followed by a game of cricket, although this time, Stan had brought two balls so that Beauty would have her own. Although Beauty still chased their ball as well, which everyone found amusing. The afternoon was enjoyed by everyone, before leaving again for Stan's place. Later that evening whilst the children had gone to bed, Stan, Jeff and Cecily were all enjoying the peace and quiet, whilst sitting on Stan's veranda. Stan and Jeff were holding a nice cool beer, whilst Cecily preferred a glass of wine. Cecily and Jeff talked about their business in Bathurst. Some land had become available next to theirs, which they had made an offer on, and hoped to expand their business. They planned to build more stables, along with another paddock to exercise the horses. Cecily spoke about Alice, saying her every spare moment was with the horses.

With her head to one side, she laughingly said, "The boys will probably prefer to work at the race track. Cars are their only interest."

Knowing the boys as he did, Stan agreed wholeheartedly. He went on to tell them about Patrick's paintings and drawings, which he had come across, continuing to say, "There are various drawings. But I think one of the paintings could be his granddad. There were other ones. And one of a woman, also a baby; they were all very good, especially for a 13-year-old. He really has an amazing talent."

Both Cecily and Jeff thought maybe the woman was Patrick's mother. Stan replied, "I did wonder that myself."

"I wonder who the baby is though," Cecily, went on to say. "Now that Patrick is settled here, maybe you could ask him a few more questions, Stan."

Stan wasn't so sure, saying, "I don't want to push him, especially as he still doesn't speak. Something must have happened to him to make him that way."

Cecily thought for a while, agreeing it was difficult, adding, "We can't ask a speech therapist either, because of the situation."

They continued to sit on the veranda, each with their own thoughts about Patrick.

Cecily pointed out, "He may have a family back in England, and they could even be searching for him. But then again, maybe his family were killed in the war, they would probably never know." Cecily looked at Stan, and asked, "Have you told Patrick, that you and I arrived here on an orphan ship?"

Stan said no, it wasn't something he had mentioned. The next day, it was decided with much excitement that they would be going to the local swimming pool. Typical of Alice, she dived into the pool as soon as they arrived, shouting, "Come on, Patrick."

Patrick who couldn't swim, hung back for a while before he carefully climbed down the steps into the shallow end. The twins followed him, not being anywhere near as brave as their sister. However, the boys and Patrick felt confident in the shallow end and were soon having fun, splashing each other, and playing tag in the water. Stan climbed into the pool to join them, throwing a beach ball for the boys to catch. It was fun, jumping up to catch the ball. Alice could see they were all having fun, so decided to join in.

Cecily and Jeff decided they would prefer to relax and just watch. After their swim, the children lay down on the grass to dry off in the sunshine, whilst Stan headed off to buy them all an ice cream. The ice creams were enjoyed in silence.

"My," said Jeff, with a laugh, "that's the quietest they've been for quite a while. Tomorrow they would be going home back to Bathurst."

Cecily and Jeff had loaded up their car with all their belongings, ready for the journey home, all of them promised to see each other again very soon.

Alice said she would write to Patrick, as soon as she got home. Stan never did speak to the postmistress; he didn't want to draw attention to Patrick, but from now on, they would write their letters to the Dubbo post office where Stan would collect them once a week. With lots of waving from the car, they drove away towards home.

Chapter 8

England

In Bletchley, Jack Taylor was relaxing at home with his parents. He was sitting opposite his dad who was hidden from view behind his newspaper. Every now and then, Jack could see wisps of smoke appearing above the paper from his dad's cigarette. Jack thought *one of these days, he was going to set his newspaper alight.*

Jack was drawn to a picture on the front page of the newspaper, quick as a flash; he reached out pulling the newspaper towards himself.

"Oh! What did you do that for."

"Sorry, Dad, but the boy in the picture looks familiar." Jack studied the picture more closely remembering that dark wet night not so long ago. *Could it be that boy?* He wondered, and it was odd how Sargent Fletcher changed the subject when Jack asked about the boy. He just assumed the boy's parents must have come to take him home.

Without hesitation, Jack contacted the police in Stony Stratford; he repeated to them everything that had happened that night. PC Bishop and PC Stewart were pleased to be finally getting somewhere with this case.

They listened to everything Jack told them. He told them about how the boy seemed traumatised and didn't speak at all; he didn't even give his name.

Jack went on to say, "Sargent Fletcher said it was a quiet night, and I could leave before the end of my shift. But before leaving, I checked on the boy again. He was still sitting on the edge of the bed, inside the cell, looking very upset, but I couldn't get him to tell me anything. I typed up a report on him and left it on my desk before going home."

After speaking to Jack, the two PCs were very keen to speak to Sargent Fletcher. They eventually sat down for an interview with Sargent Fletcher, who was annoyed with PC Jack Taylor for telling them about the boy that night. He knew he had done wrong in taking him to the Waif and Strays, and he hadn't made any effort to investigate the matter further. He had even removed the report that Jack had typed up about the incident. Sargent Fletcher knew he was in a lot of trouble now, perhaps if he came clean, it would be better for him, but he wasn't sure. He was due to retire in a few months' time and he was tired.

"The boy looked scruffy," he said, "and was alone and wouldn't speak, what was I supposed to do? I thought he was an orphan or something, and took him to an orphanage which is run by my brother Reg. It's a nice orphanage; the kids are well looked after there." The interview lasted for over an hour before PC Bishop and Stewart left along with the address of the orphanage.

As soon as he was alone, Phillip Fletcher rang his brother at the orphanage. He wanted to warn him that he was about to have a visit by the police.

Early the next day, both PCs visited the Waif and Strays. The front door was opened by a kindly looking woman, who beckoned them inside. She told them she was the matron. Leaving them in the hall, she knocked on Reg's office door. Even though he had been forewarned, he wasn't pleased to have the police in his establishment. The police sat down facing Reg Fletcher across his desk; they showed him both Patrick's school photo and the picture given to them by Patrick's granddad. He recognised the boy straight away but told the police otherwise.

"I'm sorry, constables, but I don't recognise this boy at all." Reg walked over to his filing cabinet and produced a list of the boys' names at the home from the present and going back a few years. Reg knew the police wouldn't find Patrick's name listed there. At that moment, the matron came into the office. She was carrying a tray, with a pot of tea, some sugar and milk, along with three mugs.

She set the tray down on Reg's desk. He looked up at her showing his annoyance. "Thank you, Maggie, that will be all."

As Maggie left Reg's office, she deliberately left his office door slightly open; hoping to hear something of their conversation. Unfortunately, their voices were muffled. She had always been suspicious of Reg's dealings. And even more so since three of the boys in her care had been removed without her knowledge; it was all very underhand. And Mr Thompson, the teacher, wasn't told the boys were to be taken away either. As she waited for the police to leave, she had an idea, and quickly left the building walking down to the bottom of the long drive. She waited out of sight of the orphanage for the police to appear.

As Maggie heard them approach, she stepped out and asked if she could speak to them. They pointed to their car, which was waiting in the street. She followed them over to the car; the two police officers sat in the front with Maggie sitting in the back of the car.

Maggie began, "I don't know why you wanted to speak to Reg today. But my concern is of three boys, who were here at the Waif and Strays, and then suddenly all three disappeared."

She went on to say, "Mr Thompson, the teacher, was in the middle of an arithmetic lesson, when Reg went into the classroom, saying three of the boys all had dentist appointments. He took William Dent, George Hunt and a boy who didn't speak." As soon as the matron mentioned a boy who didn't speak, their ears pricked up. "He didn't bring the boys back and we haven't seen them since."

The police asked Maggie if she could remember the date this happened.

"Yes, she said, it was 29th of April."

And could she give a description of all the boys, in particular the boy, who didn't speak? Maggie gladly described them all, also telling them about the boy who didn't speak. "He was different to the other boys who arrived at the home," she said.

"In what way was he different?" PC Stewart asked.

"Well, I could see he had been well cared for, his clothes were of good quality, and his hair was cut nicely, and although he didn't speak, he was a polite boy with good manners. Unfortunately, most of the boys who arrive at the home are the exact opposite."

PC Stewart then showed Maggie the photo, and picture of Patrick. "Oh, my goodness," she said, "Yes that's him, please tell me everything is alright."

PC Bishop then said, "Sadly, he's been missing for some time, but your information has helped us greatly. Do you have any idea of where Reg took them?"

She replied, "Reg had sent all three of them to an orphanage in Australia. Reg didn't tell me until a few weeks later, but he had personally taken them to the Port of Tilbury and put them on a ship. He said it was for a better life, with more opportunities for them, but I suspect money was involved knowing Reg."

The police were stunned at this news; it was the last thing they would have suspected. And how on earth would they break it to Sarah, and her dad, Thomas?

With heavy hearts, the police visited Sarah again to tell her about Australia. Her tears almost broke old Thomas's heart; he held her close.

"Australia," she kept saying over and over!

Thomas quietly said, "We will get him back; you mark my words, we will!"

When the police arrived back at their station, they did some investigating into Reg Fletcher. They couldn't find anything against him but arranged for him to be questioned at the station. After the questioning, they soon had the name of the ship that Patrick had sailed on. And also, the name of the orphanage he and the other boys had been sent to, in New South Wales, Australia.

It was two months later before they heard anything back from the Australian police. It transpired that Patrick didn't arrive at the orphanage. The Australian police had questioned both William Dent and George Hunt together with both boys saying how William, and the boy who didn't speak, had run away in a place called Dubbo. William was eventually caught, and taken back onto the bus, but they couldn't find the other boy anywhere. William explained he didn't see where the other boy went.

He said that he wasn't really paying attention, as he was trying to get away himself, and was very upset to have been caught. He didn't even realise that the other boy was missing at first. PC Bishop and Stewart had to break the bad news to Sarah yet again; she was heartbroken to hear Patrick hadn't been found. Simon was listening to the police talking to Sarah. He looked very sad but made no comment preferring to stay quiet as this was all his fault.

Simon was a changed man; he knew this was all his fault; the guilt was eating away at him. But the worst thing was that he had lost Sarah. She no longer spoke to him, ignoring him all the time. He had got down on his knees and said how sorry he was, but she just walked away from him.

Later in the day, after feeding Matthew, Sarah strapped him into his pushchair and walked to her dad's house. She wanted to tell him what the police had said. She broke down in tears before she could finish telling him. Thomas held her in his arms again, soothing her as best he could. Eventually, she told him what the police had said. He pulled her close again, looking into her eyes, and he said, "We must have hope, Sarah, we will find him."

Chapter 9

Bathurst Australia

Cecily was busily shopping in Bathurst. She had nearly bought everything she needed when she remembered a friend, telling her about a free dress pattern in a magazine. Cecily thought it would be lovely to make herself a new dress. She ran across the road to a newsagent, to see if she could find the magazine. Whilst she was browsing in the newsagents, her eyes were drawn to a photo, on the front of a newspaper. She covered her mouth in shock, *it's Patrick,* she thought. Patrick's picture was staring back at her.

Cecily purchased the newspaper, forgetting all about the magazine she wanted, and hurried back to her car, driving home as quickly as she could to show Jeff. Both looked at Patrick's picture again. "It's him, isn't it, Jeff?" She asked.

He nodded. "It looks that way," and together they read the story beneath the picture.

"I mentioned to Stan a while ago, that Patrick might have family looking for him. But I never expected this. What if Stan gets into trouble; it doesn't bear thinking about and he loves that boy like a father."

That very day, Cecily wrote a letter to Stan, she included the cutting of Patrick from the newspaper. Stan was whistling a tune as he walked into the post office in Dubbo. He always collected their post once a week. He had quite a handful of letters this time; he smiled to himself as he noticed the usual letter from Alice to Patrick. *Those two have become very fond of each other* he thought. Blossom had given him a list of what she needed, so he decided to buy those first, making four journeys backwards and forwards to his truck. Then he bought some clothing for Patrick, who seemed to be growing out of everything just lately. When he eventually arrived home, Patrick and Beauty were just stepping down from the veranda outside Blossom's house.

He hurried across to Stan and helped him to unload the back of his truck, carrying bits and pieces into their house. Patrick was 14 years old now and nearly as tall as Stan. Stan thought *it won't be long before he was taller than me!* They had a bite to eat, before settling in their usual chairs on their veranda, to read through the post. He could see Patrick smiling, as he read his letter from Alice.

Unfortunately, Stan had a few bills in his letters. He looked at them first, before opening the letter from Cecily. He always enjoyed her letters, but as he read through this letter, and saw the newspaper cutting, his face drained of colour. He looked across at Patrick, who had come to mean so much to him. He looked so happy these days, how on earth was he going to break this news to him, after three years? How he wished Cecily was here!

Later that night after Patrick had gone to bed, Stan took the letter and picture Cecily had sent him to show Elijah and Blossom; he wanted to discuss it with them.

Elijah read the newspaper cutting, explaining it to Blossom. Stan sat watching both Elijah and Blossom's reactions.

He told them, "I must tell Patrick when he wakes up in the morning, but I'm dreading it. Apart from his lack of speech, whatever happened to him over in England, he seems to have recovered from. He's grown into a fine young man, and I couldn't bear for him to return to a frightened little boy again."

All three talked about Patrick long into the night, but still, Stan couldn't think of what was best to do, or how to say it, he wasn't worried about himself, just Patrick, who he thought of as his son.

As usual, the next morning, they had their breakfast with Elijah and Blossom. After their breakfast, Patrick, closely followed by Beauty, walked towards the orchards. Even though the harvest had finished, there were always plenty of things to be done. The one thing Patrick loved the most was helping in the orchards. He was surprised when Stan stopped him saying, "I need to talk to you, Patrick." He looked towards Stan noticing his worried look.

Stan told Patrick to sit down. He started to pace up and down the room. Patrick was getting worried now, he hadn't seen Stan agitated like this before. Stan looked at Patrick, and said, "I have something very important to tell you, it's about your life back in England."

He patted Patrick on his shoulder, telling him, "I don't want you to worry. I don't know what happened to you, or how you came to be on the orphan ship. But I have just recently found out that your family in England are looking for you."

Patrick was shocked and clearly distressed; he didn't want to hear anymore, running from the room. He ran into one of the outbuildings, throwing himself down on the floor, he cried uncontrollably.

Stan had followed him, standing nearby waiting for the tears to subside, and he could almost feel Patrick's pain. And felt so very sorry for him, again wondering, who or what had happened to him back in England. After a while, Patrick's distress subsided; he rubbed his face with the back of his hand, his face being very red and blotchy. He noticed Stan was standing next to him, looking very concerned.

Stan was completely unaware, that Patrick had been told, he was responsible for killing his baby brother and that his dear granddad was dead. Before Patrick got upset again, Stan thought he had better get this over and done with.

"Now, I want you to listen to me, Patrick. Your picture was on the front page of a newspaper, Cecily saw it and posted it to me. It appears your mum and granddad have been searching for you, for a very long time. They had no idea, whatsoever, of you being sent to live in Australia, so it's taken them many years to trace you. There's even a picture of your mum, little brother and granddad in the paper, would you like to see it?"

Feeling slightly calmer now, but still shocked, Patrick nodded his head, following Stan back into their house. With them both sitting at the table, Stan pushed the letter from Cecily, along with the newspaper cuttings towards Patrick. He cried again when he looked at their dear faces. He then looked up at Stan with confusion written all over his face. Stan sat beside him and said, "Isn't it about time you told me everything, Patrick?"

For the first time in many years, Patrick found his voice. Although it was very shaky and quiet at first, also very emotional, the sorrow and guilt he had been carrying was finally lifted from his young shoulders. He hadn't killed his baby brother after all, and his granddad was alive and well. It took a while, with Patrick needing to stop every now and again. But after telling Stan everything that had happened, he let out a sigh of relief. But his tears started again, not for himself but for his mum and granddad, knowing what they must have gone through, and searching for him for all this while, and all because of his cruel father.

"Right," said Stan, "it looks like you and I will be sailing to England very soon." Patrick looked at Stan, and couldn't thank this man enough, for what he had done for him.

Stan said, "For now though, we need to drive into the Dubbo police station."

Patrick looked at Stan confused. "We need to let the police know you are safe, and well. And most of all, so the police can contact your family in England to tell them that you, young man, have been found at last."

Chapter 10

Both Patrick and Stan said goodbye to Elijah and Blossom. Blossom's handkerchief was wet with tears. Patrick was equally upset to leave them; he didn't know what his future would be like. Leaving Beauty behind was the hardest thing for him to do. He wrapped his arms around Beauty and buried his head into her fur; it broke the hearts of everyone watching. Elijah and Blossom promised to take good care of her until Patrick came back. Patrick hoped he would come back; he had grown to love his life here with them all, especially Stan, he looked to Stan like a father.

He felt guilty at having thoughts like that, especially when he knew of the anguish his mum and granddad must have gone through. *It must have been awful for them,* he thought. He was looking forward to going home but felt torn inside. *The best thing to do* he thought, *was talk it over with Stan,* which he did.

Stan advised him to just wait and see how he feels once he was home, and to try not to worry.

"I will be with you all the way," he said. Cecily, Jeff, Alice and the twins Ronnie and James, were all standing on the Quayside, ready to say goodbye to Stan and Patrick; their ship was getting ready to sail to England. Alice was trying very hard not to cry; she would miss Patrick so much; they had become very close over the last three years.

Patrick felt the same as Alice. At fourteen years of age, he was almost a young man and his feelings for Alice were very strong. Stan told Patrick it was time to board the ship. Patrick found himself wrapped in Cecily's arms, she kissed him. Jeff, Ronnie and James all shook his hand wishing him well. Alice didn't know what to do. But then threw herself into Patrick's arms. They held onto each other for quite a while, before Stan stepped in, and guided Patrick towards the ship's gangplank.

Finally, with a loud blast from the ship's whistle, they were on their way, with the ship slowly moving away from the Quay. Stan and Patrick were looking down from the top deck waving to everyone below. Alice waved frantically to Patrick until the ship was just a speck in the distance. Stan guided Patrick to their cabin where they unpacked. He suggested it would be a good idea to look around the ship, to familiarise themselves with where everything was. After a few days on the ship, they were both beginning to find their way around but decided it was best to stay together in case either of them got lost, as the ship was huge.

Like Patrick's previous journey on the orphan ship, he found being up on the deck the best part. Sometimes, he found himself just staring out at sea mesmerised by its vastness. He also thought about what was awaiting him back home back in England. They both whirled the time away.

With Patrick watching the sea birds overhead, he was amazed at how big they were and how they glided beautifully through the sky. He was on the lookout for an albatross.

A while ago, Stan had given Patrick a book about the albatross birds; he was fascinated by them and was scanning the blue sky to see if he could find one. Stan had made friends with another Australian man, and they would sit for hours on the deck playing card games or chess. Stan was never too far away from Patrick though, always keeping an eye on him. Not for one minute did Stan regret helping Patrick escape that day. And thank goodness, the police didn't seem concerned to investigate it any further, which was a big relief to everyone, especially Cecily. She had been very worried for Stan. One evening whilst they were both sitting on the deck looking up at the stars, Stan thought it was time to tell Patrick that he and Cecily had been orphans.

"Cecily and I lost our parents when we were just babies," he said. "We were far too young to remember them. We were eventually placed in an orphanage, but luckily for us, we were adopted by a lovely couple who became our new parents." Stan told Patrick their names were, Charles and Margaret Smith.

He went on to tell Patrick that they ran a successful fruit and vegetable store, but were thinking of emigrating to either Canada or Australia. However, they chose Australia settling in Bathurst, and opened another fruit and vegetable store there. "Our father was a clever man; he invested wisely in other business. But sadly, as they grew older, they both died quite close together. We all had a wonderful life together. They also left me and Cecily well provided for. Cecily purchased the stables and the smallholding, and I purchased the almond orchard."

Patrick was listening quietly. He understood why Stan had told him about his adoption; it explained Stan's compassion towards himself. Their voyage was coming to an end, with the weather becoming much cooler although it was the month of

July. Stan and Patrick were looking out from the top deck, as the coast of England came ever closer. With the Quay becoming visible, Patrick felt happy, but anxious at the same time. Once the ship had docked, they both picked up their belongings, making their way to the gangplank.

Stan had instructions to go directly towards a particular area, where he and Patrick would be met by PC Pete Bishop and PC Kate Stewart. After all their hard work in tracing Patrick, the two PCs had been granted permission to meet the ship. All four of them greeted each other warmly, with both PCs being so pleased to have found Patrick at last. Some press photographers were there, jostling with each other for the best photo. The police ushered them away from the press and towards their car.

Within two hours, the car pulled up outside Patrick's house. As he opened the car door, he could see his mum with her arms outstretched running towards him. The tears were pouring down both of their faces as they fell into each other's arms. Sarah held onto him tightly, as if she never wanted to let him go. Over his mum's shoulder, he could see his dear granddad, looking a lot older. He reached out to him, and they held each other for a long time. "Oh, lad," he said, "I'm that pleased to have you back!"

The spell was soon broken, when a little voice asked, "Are you my big brother?" Patrick looked down, and there stood little Matthew looking up at him, not a baby anymore.

Patrick knelt to him and said, "Yes, I am your big brother."

Matthew lifted his arms up towards Patrick to be picked up; Patrick did so and held his little chest close to his own.

Matthew said, "Would like to see my train set?" making everyone smile. Patrick turned towards Stan, who stepped forward to shake hands with Sarah and Thomas.

Thomas ushered everyone inside, saying, "Come along, everyone, we have some very nice cake waiting to be eaten."

Everyone went into the house, including the two smiling PCs. Everyone gathered in Sarah's kitchen. It was a lovely happy gathering, with lots of chatter and hugging again. Sarah could hardly believe Patrick was standing next to her, after all this time. And neither Sarah nor Thomas could get over how tall he was, and he looked so well. Sarah turned towards Stan. "I can't thank you enough for your kindness, Stan, and for bringing Patrick back home to us."

Stan replied, "He's a fine boy, and I don't regret the day we happened to find each other."

He also couldn't help but notice how lovely Sarah was, with her petite figure and lovely blonde hair, so like Patrick's. Although her eyes were blue, Patrick's were a deep brown.

Thomas looked towards Stan, saying, "You have a big heart, Stan. How can we ever thank you?"

He shook Stan's hand again and again. "I'm looking forward to getting to know you as well, and to hearing all about your orchards and that big country of yours."

The two PCs had thoroughly enjoyed bringing Patrick home but said they needed to get back to their station. With everyone thanking them, they left the house saying they would call again, in a few days' time, adding that Jack Taylor might be calling in to see Patrick.

Jack, they said, was the first officer to recognise Patrick's picture in the newspaper. Mind you, little did they know it would lead them to Australia. When the officers had left,

Patrick turned to his mum to ask where his father was. Although he was dreading facing him again, Patrick thought it was odd that he wasn't there.

Sarah hugged Patrick again, saying, "Your father thought it best to wait and see you later today when everyone has gone home. He didn't want to spoil your homecoming. After what happened that night, he's changed from how you would remember him, Patrick. It took me a very long time to forgive him for what happened that night. But I did eventually after we were told he was suffering from battle fatigue. Unfortunately, the battle fatigue changed him, making him very agitated and difficult. You will notice a big change in him."

Patrick looked confused, asking his mum what battle fatigue was. Sarah tried to think of how she could describe it to Patrick, without causing him to worry. "It's a kind of anxiety after the war," she said, "it made him very sad. It was your granddad who suggested that your father might benefit from seeing a doctor. About two weeks after that awful night you went missing, your father became very agitated. He insisted he didn't need a doctor at first, but finally gave in. He has medication now, and a new job which doesn't cause him any worry."

Sarah didn't want to worry Patrick by telling him the truth, not yet anyway, but things were not the same between her and Simon now and never would be; what he did was unforgivable.

Patrick still felt nervous about seeing his father again but didn't say anymore. Just at that moment, they were joined by Percy Pearce. He knocked at their door and stepped inside at the same time. Walking across the room, he embraced Patrick in his strong arms. Percy was a big kind-hearted man with an even bigger personality.

"Goodness me," he said, "you have grown, Patrick." He embraced Partick again and said, "Welcome home, my boy."

Percy also turned towards Stan. "So, you're the man we are indebted to, shaking his hand up and down."

And with a big smile on his face, Percy turned and left their house, saying he would be back later to take Thomas home.

Later that same evening, with little Matthew tucked up in his bed, Patrick, told everyone a little more about his life in Australia, smiling broadly as he told them about Stan buying him a puppy, who he had named Beauty.

"She's quite a big dog now though," said Patrick with pride, "and so intelligent, every night she sleeps at the bottom of my bed."

He also told them about Elijah and Blossom, explaining, "They also live on Stan's property and are looking after Beauty for me."

Sarah and Thomas felt a little alarmed by the way Patrick spoke; he obviously loved his life in Australia. At that moment, Percy returned to take Thomas home. Thomas turned to Stan, saying, "I hope you don't mind Stan, but you will be staying at my house whilst you're here."

Stan said he didn't mind at all, and it was very kind of Thomas to offer his home like that.

After saying goodnight to Sarah and Patrick, Stan followed Thomas and Percy outside to Percy's van. His van displayed, Percy meat Pearce, on both sides of his van, which made Stan chuckle.

"It's just a short journey to my house," explained Thomas, "but ever since I sprained my ankle quite a while ago, I can't seem to walk as far as I used to."

Patrick remained sitting next to his mum in the living room. He looked around the room noticing it hadn't changed at all; everything was just as he remembered it. Sarah wanted to ask him so many questions, but at the same time, she didn't want to bombard him. Instead, she put her arm around him and said, "Why don't you tell me a little more about Beauty?"

"Well," said Patrick with a smile as he thought of Beauty. "She's very sweet-natured and loyal. When Stan first got her, she was just a bundle of fur and kept chewing things. She can be naughty sometimes though, especially if she sees a kangaroo, she barks at them a lot, but they don't take any notice of her. Stan showed me how to train her, which was difficult at first, Mum, because I couldn't speak."

Sarah had been told about that by the police, which was very upsetting to hear. Sarah explained to Patrick, how the police had told her about his speech problem. And how very sad she was to hear that. "The police also told me it was due to the trauma you had experienced."

She felt the tears coming again, this time, it was Patrick who comforted her. "Oh, Patrick! When I think of what you've been through, it's all so dreadful. I knew your father was difficult but I had no idea of how cruel he was to you. I feel so guilty for not noticing his behaviour. How could a mother not know?"

Patrick patted her knee. "I'm here now, Mum, and it's best to try and put it behind us."

Just at that moment, they heard the front door open. His father walked into the room and stood in front of Patrick. At first, they just looked at one another. He leaned towards Patrick with tears running down his face, he asked Patrick to forgive him.

Still, Patrick wasn't sure of what to say, he wished Stan and his granddad were still there. All he could think of to say was, "I'm sorry to hear you have been ill, Father."

Simon made no comment but continued to look towards Patrick. Sarah felt unsure of what to say as well. So, she asked Patrick about his sea voyage. He explained the journey as best he could, explaining the huge expanse of the ocean, and the different countries he had seen on the way home, adding how much he had enjoyed the voyage. Patrick felt uncomfortable under his father's gaze, but realised it was early days yet, after all, he had only just got home. It had been a long day, and Patrick was feeling weary, he looked at his mum and asked if she minded if he went to bed.

"Of course not, Patrick. Come on, let's get you settled for the night."

Sarah followed Patrick into his old bedroom; he looked around noticing this room hadn't changed either. It was as if the room was waiting for him to come home. The easel his granddad had made for him still stood in one corner, along with his favourite books. To Patrick, it all seemed so long ago, he felt like a different person now. Sarah embraced him again, saying, "I don't want to let you out of my sight ever again."

Patrick smiled, and said, "See you in the morning, mum." As he lay in his old bed, he did indeed feel very tired, but couldn't seem to sleep. He missed Beauty; he looked towards the bottom of his bed, wishing Beauty was cuddled up there, and he wondered how she was. Then he thought of Alice and decided he would write her a long letter in the morning. The next morning, Patrick found himself sitting at the kitchen table; he was having breakfast with a very inquisitive Matthew. His little brother had poached eggs all around his mouth, which he was completely unaware of. Instead, he was intent on asking lots of questions, which were mostly about Beauty.

It soon became obvious to Patrick that Matthew was yearning for a puppy; he wanted to know how big Beauty was, and what colour she was, on and on he went asking questions. Patrick answered all of his questions as best as he could, finding his little brother quite charming in all his innocence. "I have some drawings of Beauty inside my luggage. Would you like to see them?"

Matthew nodded his head and clapped his hands at the same time. "Oh, yes please," he said and was about to follow Patrick up to his bedroom before Sarah called him back.

"Have you forgotten something, Matthew?" He looked puzzled. Before realising he had what remained of his breakfast still around his mouth, he stood still next to his mum whilst she cleaned him up with a flannel. He then laughed and excitedly followed Patrick from the kitchen.

Patrick pulled out various drawings he had of Beauty; some of her as a puppy, and some of how she looked, just before Patrick left her.

"Oh," said Matthew, "I wish I could have a dog just like her, but father won't let me."

Patrick gently asked him why that was and Matthew sighed. "It's because he isn't very well."

Patrick asked his mum a little more about his father. She sighed, saying, "It took many weeks before we realised something wasn't quite adding up, about the night you went missing. Your granddad was very suspicious of your father hiding something, so between us, we tackled him about it. At first, he was very dismissive of any wrongdoing. The police also asked him lots of questions; unfortunately, your father became very agitated. But gradually over the weeks, he became very withdrawn. It was then that your granddad thought he should see a doctor. Of course, your father refused, so your granddad and I spoke to Dr Williams."

"He was very kind and visited your father at home. He was here for a long time, and he diagnosed the battle fatigue. It was obvious he was struggling at work as well, and that's where Percy helped. He offered your father a job delivering to his rural customers. Of course, he wasn't keen at first. But I persuaded him to give it a try, and it's worked out well so far. We owe such a lot to Percy; he's been such a good friend."

The days quickly went by, with various visitors wanting to see Patrick. Mary, their next-door neighbour, could hardly wait to see him again.

"Oh, Patrick," she said. "I can't say how pleased I am to see you safe and sound and to think you found yourself all that way away in Australia. It's like something you would read in a book, not right next door."

She stayed for a little while longer, enjoying a cup of tea with both Patrick and his mum.

She asked if he liked being in Australia. Patrick replied that he did like it and that he missed his dog, Beauty. They all chatted for quite some time before Mary left for her own house. At the front door, she turned and reached up cupping Patrick's face in between her hands, saying again, how lovely it was to have him back.

After Mary left, Patrick told his mum he was going to call on his friend Robert. As Patrick walked to where Robert lived, the area didn't feel quite as familiar as it used to do, everything felt strange. He knocked on Robert's front door. It was opened by Robert's mum; she put her hand to her mouth, "Oh my goodness, it's Patrick."

She beckoned for him to come in, whilst shouting to everyone, "Patrick is here." Robert's two older sisters were the first to appear. Maggie and Hazel at first just gapped at Patrick; it didn't go unnoticed by them that he had grown tall and handsome.

Patrick was starting to feel uncomfortable until Robert appeared from behind them. "Let me get through, you two," he said, pushing them out of his way.

Both Robert and Patrick shook hands warmly, "It's so good to see you, Patrick," he said. "Come on through into the kitchen where we can sit in peace," telling his big sisters to go away. The two of them chatted for hours, catching up on just about everything. Before Robert could ask Patrick what happened, Patrick explained what happened the night he went missing, telling him about his father, and how shocked, and upset he was and couldn't seem to speak. He hung his head, telling Robert his father had accused him of killing baby Matthew, and his granddad was dead.

"I must have been deeply shocked, which triggered some sort of trauma, I couldn't seem to speak. I just couldn't believe my father would say that to me, after all, I was only eleven at the time." He shrugged his shoulders and said, "So that's why it was so difficult to find me, no one knew who I was, because I couldn't speak."

Robert had heard some gossip about what happened and felt so very shocked by what Patrick had told him. How on earth could Sergeant Smithers, have done that to Patrick, or to anyone? Patrick went on to explain his father was suffering from battle fatigue, which had made him act strangely. Robert had his own thoughts on the matter, but Patrick was here now, and looking well. He asked him about the orphanage he found himself in. Patrick assured him it wasn't too bad. "There were only twelve of us boys," he said, "we had school lessons, went to church sometimes, and the matron there was kind, and so was the teacher, so I guess, we were all very lucky. Reg Fletcher though wasn't so nice. He was the man who ran the orphanage, and it was he who arranged for us to join the migrant programme to Australia."

Patrick went on to tell Robert all about his life in Australia on Stan's property, and the almond orchards. Robert thought Australia sounded wonderful. Patrick laughed; he could remember Robert being frightened of a grass snake, they once saw. So, he told him all about the snakes in Australia, which made Robert wince. They laughed together about that.

Robert asked if Patrick would like to come along to a youth club with him. "It's on Thursday evening," he said. "In the village hall, it's just nice to meet up with people your own age."

Patrick said he would enjoy that and would call around for him on Thursday, in time for the youth club. It wasn't long before Jack Taylor also wanted to visit Patrick. Jack had peddled his bike all the way to Stony Stratford, from his home in Bletchley, arriving at the Smither's front door feeling very hot and thirsty. He thought, *thank goodness*, I'm not wearing my police uniform; I would have been even hotter in that, he suddenly thought *I hope Patrick is at home. It was a jolly long way to peddle.*

Luckily for Jack, Patrick was just walking back home from Robert's house. As Patrick turned into Church Street, he could see a young man knocking on his front door; Sarah had answered the door, just as Patrick approached. Jack had no idea he was standing next to Patrick, and Patrick didn't recognise him either. It wasn't until Sarah asked how Robert was, that the penny dropped with Jack.

Well, I never, he thought. The tall young man standing in front of him was nothing like the frightened boy he had looked after that night. Jack could remember it all so vividly. He introduced himself to them. Sarah asked him if he would like to come inside the house.

Jack said could he leave his bike leaning against their house. Sarah assured him that would be alright. Jack followed Patrick and Sarah into her kitchen, where she made cool drinks for them all, smiling when Jack drank his straight down. "My goodness, you were thirsty," she said, before making him another one.

Jack explained he had just peddled his bike all the way from Bletchley. "That is a long way," remarked Patrick.

Jack looked at Patrick and said, "I was on duty at the police station the night we found you, of course, we didn't know your name then."

He went on to tell them. "It was me who found you walking down the road that night. It was dark and raining very hard, and you were wet through, looking so sad and dejected. It was tempting to take you home to my mum to be looked after," he said with a smile. "But anyway," said Jack, "I'm so pleased to see you looking so well again, and back home with your family. In fact, I didn't even recognise you earlier; you look nothing like the boy from that night. And I've heard it's been quite a journey. In fact, if it wasn't for the circumstances, it would have been an adventure!"

Patrick laughed at that, he liked Jack; he was a nice down-to-earth sort of chap.

"I'm sorry that I can't remember very much about that night, Jack, but thank you for all you did. PC Bishop and PC Stewart told me all that happened that night. And how it was you, who found me walking along the road." Patrick then said, "Oh, I've just realised, it was you who recognised my picture in the newspaper, wasn't it?"

Jack said, "Yep, one and the same. And my dad has repeated it to everyone at his local pub everyone who will listen that is," which made them all laugh.

Sarah told him, "You have the makings of a fine policeman, Jack."

Jack thanked her, saying, "Well, I best be on my way home."

Both Patrick and Sarah walked with Jack to their front door. Patrick asked him to call again anytime he was in Stony Stratford. Jack said he would like that. Just as he was about to peddle off, a car pulled up and out jumped two men.

Like Jack before them, they introduced themselves, one was a reporter and the other a photographer. The reporter wanted to know if he could ask Patrick a few questions. Patrick hadn't been prepared for all this attention; he turned to his mum a bit unsure. But Jack stepped in, saying, "How about just a photo for now?" explaining who he was at the same time.

The photographer obliged, taking photos of Patrick, Sarah and Jack. The journalist told them he was going to add Jack Taylor had the qualities of a fine young police officer.

"My dad really will have something to show off about now," said Jack, leaving everyone laughing as he peddled away on his bike.

Patrick said, "Phew! I didn't expect all of this, Mum."

"Neither did I," she said.

"Mum, what time will you be collecting Matthew from his nursery school?"

"In half an hour. Are you coming with me?"

"Yes, please. Although perhaps I should wear a hat and a false beard or something."

With that, they both left the house laughing together. Stan was enjoying his stay in England. Although he had been born somewhere in Gloucestershire, he didn't know very much about it. Both he and Cecily were just small babies at the time.

Stan was particularly enjoying the company of Thomas, and could understand why Patrick thought so much of his granddad; he was a very kindly man. Thomas had made Stan feel very welcome. The room he was sleeping in was very comfortable. From the window, Stan had a nice view of Thomas's garden, along with the chickens strutting around their coop. It was all so very different to Stan's property, *everywhere was so much smaller and quaint in comparison* he thought. Like Patrick though, he missed Beauty. She was a lovely dog to have around, although he knew she would be well looked after by Elijah and Blossom. He hoped she wasn't pining too much for Patrick.

Just then Patrick arrived at his granddad's house, along with Matthew and his mum. With everyone looking on, Patrick took Matthew's hand, and showed him how to feed the chickens, just like he used to do. Matthew wasn't so sure; he hadn't shown any interest in the chickens before. But since Patrick had arrived home, Matthew followed him everywhere; he greatly admired his big brother. Gently, Patrick showed Matthew into the chicken coop; he chuckled as the chickens pecked at his shoes, just as Patrick used to do, making everyone laugh. Patrick also showed Matthew where the eggs would be.

He was overjoyed to have collected four eggs, he ran from the chicken coop to show his mum.

"My goodness," said Sarah, "what clever chickens."

He asked, "Can we have them for breakfast tomorrow, mum?"

"Of course, you can!"

"And Patrick can help me to smash them."

Sarah laughed. "You mean, can you scramble them?" She said.

They were all enjoying being in Thomas's garden. Patrick showed Stan the various vegetables his granddad grew, and the few fruit trees he had. All so very different from what Stan was used to. After a while, it started to rain, with everyone running back inside the house. They settled down to a cup of tea and milk for Matthew. Stan started to tell them all about his property in Australia, helped along by Patrick, who tried to describe the almond-shaking machine. Neither Sarah nor Thomas had ever heard of such a machine. Patrick went over to Granddad's cupboard where he kept all manner of things. He found some pencils and paper and carefully drew the almond shaker for them all to see; everyone was watching as Patrick drew his picture.

Thomas and Sarah smiled at how his tongue still peeped out, just like it used to. When Patrick had finished, Thomas was astounded. "My goodness," he said, "that's a machine and a half," and he asked how many almond trees Stan had.

Stan scratched his head, "Well, I've never counted them all. I guess, it's thousands."

It was hard for anyone other than Stan or Patrick to visualise the sheer expanse of Stan's property. Patrick told them how beautiful the trees looked, when they had their blossom, some were white whereas others were a pale pink.

Again, Sarah and Thomas looked towards each other thinking the same thing about Patrick; it was worrying them.

On Sunday, When Percy's butcher shop was closed, he kindly lent his delivery van to Stan so that he could explore the different places in their area. Patrick went along with him, and so did Matthew, feeling very grown up sitting next to his big brother in Percy's van.

Sarah had packed them a picnic to share, and waved until they were out of sight. They drove off into the countryside, which wasn't very far away. Patrick pointed out various places, where he used to play with Robert. They stopped by the stream for a while, Patrick wanted to show them where he and Robert loved to fish. He pointed out a spinney where they quite often played hide and seek as well. Stan couldn't help to notice how green everywhere looked, compared to where he lived; the English countryside was truly beautiful.

He happily drove on whistling a tune, with the boys looking out for somewhere nice to stop and eat their picnic.

Patrick suggested they drive to Woburn. "It is beautiful there," he said, "with lots of places we can enjoy our picnic."

Matthew was frowning. "Is that very far?" He asked. "I'm getting hungry."

Patrick laughed and assured him it wasn't very far away.

They soon arrived in Woburn. Whilst driving through the small town, Stan remarked on how pretty the town was. "I thought Stony Stratford was a pretty place, and this one is too, although much smaller."

Patrick thought just the same, with the sandstone buildings looking so pretty in the sunshine. He pointed out the correct road for Stan to follow, which would lead them to Woburn Woods. A little voice piped up, "Are we there yet? I'm still hungry. And mum has made my favourite sandwiches."

With both Stan and Patrick smiling at little Matthew, they pulled into a side road and stopped the van. Walking just a little way into the woods, Stan found a nice spot for them to sit.

He spread out the picnic blanket for them to sit down. Straight away, Matthew started to rummage in the picnic basket for the sandwiches. "See," he said, "egg and cress sandwiches, my favourite."

Patrick had come to realise that all the food was Matthew's favourite. *He was one adorable little boy*, thought Patrick. "And look," Said Mathew with his mouth full of sandwiches, "Mum has made a cake as well."

Patrick asked him if it was his favourite cake. "Of course, it is, silly," he said, which made them all laugh again.

After they had eaten every crumb, they packed everything away inside the van and went for a walk into the woods. Stan was enjoying every moment, looking up at all the different trees, some small and some large. Patrick told Stan he used to come here a lot at one time, especially when Granddad used to have a car, but he preferred not to drive anymore.

"Didn't your father bring you?" Stan asked.

Patrick just said, "No, he didn't."

All three walked on a little further until Matthew complained his legs were tired. With that, Stan picked him up and sat him on his shoulders.

"Oh! Look at me," said Matthew, looking down at Patrick, "I'm taller than you now, Patrick." Patrick smiled and told him he was a little monkey.

"You mean, like a monkey like in the Tarzan books?"

"Yes, just like that, you might even grow a long curly tail too."

His little brother was quite a character he thought.

They came across a tree trunk lying on the ground, which made a nice seat for a little rest. Patrick looked around at the beautiful scenery, saying he wished he had his sketchbook with him. He loved how the sunlight shone through the trees, changing their colours.

"Perhaps if we ask Percy nicely, he will lend us his van again next Sunday," said Stan.

Although it was his day off work, Simon didn't usually like Sundays, but today was different. With both the boys going out with that bloke Stan, he had Sarah all to himself, which cheered him a little.

He decided as soon as he saw Stan, he didn't like him; the man was far too nice for his liking. Everyone seemed to like Stan, which annoyed Simon. It hadn't gone unnoticed either that Sarah seemed to think he was the bee's knees. *Anyway*, he thought, *what will we do today?* He found Sarah in the kitchen. She was just about to make a salad for later that day.

Simon stood watching her for a while, thinking how lucky he was that she stood by him with everything that happened with Patrick. He seemed oblivious to the fact that she was finding it increasingly difficult and was unhappy.

He still found it hard to have a great deal to do with the boy, even with little Matthew. He couldn't seem to be the loving father he knew he should be. He found himself having to pretend to be what he wasn't, but then he shrugged his shoulders telling himself not all fathers are perfect.

He asked Sarah if she would like to go for a walk somewhere. She told him that she intended to visit her dad.

Simon's face clouded over, but he quickly masked it with a smile. "In that case, I will come with you," he said. Sarah showed her surprise. "Well," he said, "it's a lovely day for a walk in the sunshine."

He wanted to be alone with her, and if they had to visit Thomas on the way, so be it. He would make sure they didn't stay too long. Sarah could see he was trying hard and said that would be nice. Whilst Sarah went to change her clothes into what she called her Sunday best, Simon walked quickly down to the bottom of their garden. He looked around to make sure he wasn't being watched, then carefully squeezed his arm behind the garden shed, soon feeling with his fingers what he wanted.

Smiling to himself, he lifted out his bottle of vodka. He looked around again, before putting the bottle to his lips, taking a good gulp, followed by another. Wiping his mouth on the back of his hand, he placed the bottle back in his hiding place. As he went back into the house, he felt inside his pockets for his chewing gum. He knew it would help mask the smell of the alcohol; his cigarettes seemed to help as well.

Sarah had noticed the chewing gum a few times and asked Simon why all of a sudden he seemed so fond of it, she didn't like it at all. He told her it helped to settle his nerves. She seemed to accept that and didn't mention it again.

When Sarah reappeared, she looked very pretty in a blue skirt with a white blouse, and a blue cardigan over her shoulders in case it turned cool. Simon stood to attention beside her, holding out his arm, saying, "Is madam ready?"

She smiled, putting her arm through his, setting off to visit Thomas. Both enjoyed their walk towards Thomas's house. Sarah remarked what a lovely day it was, and said she hoped Matthew and Patrick were enjoying their time showing Stan around the countryside.

"I packed them a lovely picnic," she continued to say, "I wonder where they will stop to eat it." Simon listened to her talking about her boys all the way to Thomas's house. He responded now and then, but his responses were half-hearted. Thomas was pleased to see Sarah, and very surprised to see Simon walk in with her, although Simon acted like a devoted husband and father, Thomas wasn't so sure. But he felt guilty, thinking of the war that Simon had been involved in, and the problems he was having now.

Thomas couldn't help noticing Simon's speech was slightly slurred. He wondered if he had heard correctly, so he listened more carefully, and sure enough, he was talking slightly slurred. He told himself it must be the medication he had been prescribed.

I've got to give him the benefit of the doubt, he thought. As it was such a lovely day, they all went into the garden; Thomas offered them his homemade lemonade.

Sarah said, "Oh! This is lovely, Dad. You must give me the recipe." Thomas tapped the side of his nose telling her it was a secret. Sarah giggled. "Oh, Dad," she said.

Simon played along, but found it all rather tedious; he stood up saying, "Come along, my dear. You promised me a walk in the sunshine."

Sarah said goodbye to her dad; she hadn't noticed Simon's irritation. But it didn't go unnoticed by Thomas. Thomas walked with them to his garden gate and waved them off. Then he walked slowly back inside his house, feeling very concerned, things were still not quite right with Simon.

The two of them walked towards the park. Simon was pleased to have Sarah to himself once again, well, for a while anyway, he thought. Finding an unoccupied bench, they sat down feeling the sun on both their faces. Simon thinking again, how pretty Sarah looked this afternoon, he tentatively put his arm around her shoulder, expecting her to rest her head on his, but she didn't. After a while, she looked at him asking if he was still enjoying his new job.

"Oh yes," he said, and proceeded to tell her about some of the strange characters, he met whilst doing his deliveries.

He mentioned one lady, who he said frightened him half to death. "She only has one tooth in her head, and just a few whips of long white hair, which sprouts out just above her ears."

She found that very funny and was in fits of laughter, he liked to hear her laugh. *His Sarah* he thought *his and no one else's.* They left the park, and began to walk home, he took her hand and held it tight in his own. Sarah wanted to pull her hand away. Pretending all was well between them, was becoming a strain for her. Simon was pleased to have his meat delivery job, although he wasn't quite as keen on Percy Pearce as everyone else seemed to be. He found it odd when he met Percy's wife; compared to Percy, she was a small quiet woman. He wondered how on earth she put up with him.

He found his jovial personality annoying, but still, he was grateful for the delivery job, in more ways than one. Firstly, he enjoyed having the van to drive around in, and being alone; he preferred his own company. But mostly, he was his own boss; no one asked questions if he deviated away from the areas he was supposed to deliver in, which came in very handy when he stopped to buy his vodka. He made sure to use different places, and times of the day to buy his drink, quite often stopping in quiet places to take a good gulp.

He knew he shouldn't be drinking vodka, along with his medication, but his craving was so strong, Sometimes, he felt guilty; he knew Sarah would be disappointed in him.

But then, he told himself, he wasn't hurting anyone, and she wasn't likely to know, he would make sure she never did. Whilst he was driving down a particular country lane, he noticed an old disused cow shed. He pulled over for a closer look, thinking, it could be the ideal place to hide a bottle of vodka or two. He had a good look around the shed.

Seeing it hadn't been used in a very long time, it was full of cobwebs and birds' droppings, it even looked like bats roosted there during the day. He climbed back into the van, feeling very pleased with himself for finding yet another hiding place. Stan's time in England was going by quickly.

He had thoroughly enjoyed his stay; he particularly enjoyed the company of Thomas. It had been noticed that Thomas's friend Percy, had been a godsend to the family, especially whilst Patrick was missing, it must have been a dreadful time, for both Sarah and Thomas.

And how Sarah could ever forgive Simon, he would never know, but had she? But Stan couldn't help to notice things were not as they seemed between Sarah and Simon. But how could you ever forgive what he had said and done? Stan was horrified when Patrick finally found his voice to tell him. That poor boy had kept it bottled up inside him for so long; to look at him now, you would never believe what he had been through.

He looked like a tall and confident young man, so different to the frightened little boy he found that day in the back of his truck. Stan knew saying goodbye to Patrick, when he returned to Australia, was going to be one of the hardest things he had ever done. Patrick went with his mum to collect Matthew from the nursery. It was in the church hall, which was just across the road from their house. When Matthew came out, he ran straight to Patrick. He picked him up and swung him around, much to Matthew's delight.

Putting him down again, Patrick asked him what he had done at his nursery that day. Matthew furrowed his brows, thinking about the question. "Well," he said, "I had a biscuit and a cup of milk."

"No," said Patrick, "did you play any games?"

"Well, we played with some plasticine, and I made some wriggly worms with it, and then the teacher read us a story."

With that, Patrick took his hand, saying, "Come on, we are going to visit Granddad now, then you can tell him all about your wriggly worms."

Sarah followed behind smiling at them both. Matthew asked if Stan would be there. "Most certainly," replied Patrick. They arrived at Granddad's house, just as he had finished making a fresh jug of his lemonade. Everyone went out into the garden to enjoy the sunshine and the lemonade. Stan was pleased to see Patrick; he patted him on the back and asked how he was getting on. He told Stan he had been to see Robert, and how good it was to see him again. He went on to tell Stan that Robert looked just the same, although they had grown taller. He was just the same old Robert!

"We talked for ages, mostly when we were little, and at school together. Then he told me how awful he felt when I went missing, and how he was asked by the police to show them where we used to play."

Patrick frowned, "I feel bad to think of so many people being worried about me." Stan put his arm around his shoulder.

"It was a dreadful thing that happened to you, Patrick. We just have to be thankful that, eventually everything worked out well, and going forward is what's important now."

Patrick smiled at that, and said, "That's just what Granddad said. I had a visit from Jack Taylor as well. He was the policeman who found me wandering along the road that night."

Patrick smiled again as he thought of Jack. "He was ever such a nice chap, Stan, and he has promised to call in again. I shall look forward to that. Oh! And Robert has asked me about going to a youth club with him. It's on Thursday evening. He says it's good fun and interesting."

Stan was pleased that Patrick was looking happy, and starting to settle in at home again. The two of them were being watched by Sarah. She wished Simon would talk to Patrick as Stan did. It made her feel sad to think of Simon. She knew he was still difficult towards Patrick, and he wasn't very interested in Matthew either. She felt her gaze fall on Stan. He had the qualities that Simon didn't. Sarah admired Stan for his compassion and kindness towards Patrick. Or was it something else, she wasn't sure; she just liked him, that's all. At that moment, Stan turned and saw Sarah was looking at him. He smiled back at her; she blushed like a schoolgirl and looked away.

Thomas noticed the looks between them, and thought *oh heck! That will put the cat amongst the pigeons, that's for sure.*

Thomas called out to Patrick, "Let's get the cricket bat out of the shed and have a game of cricket."

It wasn't long before everyone was enjoying themselves. Sarah kicked off her shoes to run after the ball when it came her way. Matthew wanted to win but sulked when he was caught out. So, Stan threw him over his shoulder which made him giggle. Thomas said he would be the wicketkeeper, as he couldn't run around like the rest of them did; everyone was having such good fun until it started to rain. Laughing together, they all ran back inside the house.

"That was fun," said Stan, "and you, little Matthew played well," as he tickled him. Again, Sarah's eyes were drawn towards Stan. She couldn't help but wonder why he was a single man; he obviously enjoyed being part of a family.
Stan looked up; their eyes met again. Sarah's, large and blue; Stan's also, blue with crinkles around the edges. They held each other's gaze for a while. Suddenly the moment was broken; someone was knocking on Thomas's front door.
It was Percy standing there along with his wife Judith.

"We were just walking past your house," he told Thomas, "as it started to rain. So, we thought we would shelter here, is that alright with you, Thomas?" as he patted him on his back.

Everyone smiled, that was just like Percy. To invite himself in. He reached out to shake Stan's hand and Patrick's not forgetting little Matthew, and bowed to Sarah, making her smile.

Sarah went off into the kitchen to make everyone a drink. She found some cake in one of her dad's cupboards, along with some biscuits, and was about to put them on a plate when Stan appeared in the kitchen doorway. "Is there anything I can help you with?" He asked.

Sarah tried not to, but she blushed again. "Perhaps you could take the plate of cake and biscuits, into everyone," she said.

As he took the plate from her, their fingers touched. He held her gaze for a few moments before going back into the living room. Everyone in the living room seemed to be talking at once, which was a relief for Stan. He sat down quietly to gather his thoughts. After all these years, of one day hoping to find a beautiful exceptional woman like Sarah.

And I go and find her across the other side of the world, and to top it off, she just happens to be married.

Stan's thoughts were interrupted by Matthew. He was pulling at his shirt to get his attention. "Will you play snap with me, please, Stan?"

"Well," said Stan, "since you asked so nicely, how can I refuse?" Matthew climbed up to the table and waited for Stan to shuffle the cards. Whilst Stan and Matthew were playing snap, he was looking across at Sarah, who was happily chatting to Judith. They were discussing dress material. Judith asked Sarah if she could make her a new dress. It was for a dance she and Percy were going to.

Sarah said, of course, she would. She liked Judith; she was a kindly person, just like her husband Percy.

"The dance is in two weeks' time though," said Judith, "sorry, I have left it a bit late."

"In that case," said Sarah, "I had better get you measured up very soon."

That very evening, Judith arrived at Sarah's house along with her dress material, and a new dress pattern she had chosen from their local haberdashery shop, along the high street. Sarah took her up to her tiny sewing room; she soon had Judith's measurements, saying she would cut out the pattern that very evening. Admiring the material Judith had chosen, it was a lovely dusky pink, and almost shimmered in the light. Judith asked, "Why don't you and Simon come to the dance?" Sarah knew what Simon's answer would be to that, but promised to ask him.

"You are both very welcome to sit with us, at our table if you do decide to come," she said.

The next day, Sarah did mention the dance to Simon. She told him they had been invited to sit with Percy and his wife Judith. Simon pulled a mocking face and was completely uninterested. A few days later, Judith arrived again at Sarah's house for her final dress fitting; she was delighted with it.

"I can't thank you enough," she said. The hem needed to be altered, which Sarah did whilst Judith waited armed with a cup of tea.

"Did you ask Simon about the dance, Sarah?"

"I did, thank you but no, he doesn't think it's quite his thing these days."

"That's a shame, why don't you ask that nice Australian man instead?" Sarah smiled, saying she would think about it.

Stan had just three more days to go before returning to Australia. He wanted to spend as much time with Patrick as he could. He knew Patrick was feeling torn; he loved his family here and understood the anguish they had been put through. He also felt guilty knowing how much he missed Alice and Beauty, not to mention everyone else, and Australia; how he loved that great big country.

Then there was the closeness that both Stan and Patrick had between them. Stan knew without Patrick saying anything, he had become like a father figure to him.

Oh! He thought, *why was life so difficult sometimes?*

In his own way, Stan was trying to take Patrick's mind off his departure, by keeping him busy. Firstly, he encouraged him to sketch as many pictures as he could.

Sketches of the places they had both visited whilst Stan was staying there and of his house and family, telling him Elijah and Blossom would love to see those. Patrick also wrote letters to Cecily and Jeff, not forgetting the twins Ronnie and James. He told them all about a new race track, that had recently opened near to where he lived.

'It's called Silverstone,' he wrote, 'and one of these days, I hope to go there, to see the racing,' and he included two sketches of racing cars for them. Lastly, he wrote a very long letter to Alice, goodness knows how he would miss her!
Alice was like bright colours he thought, full of life, vibrant and dazzling. Then there was Beauty; he certainly couldn't write her a letter he thought.

It hurt to think he couldn't cuddle her, feel her warm fur against his face, or laugh when she barked at kangaroos. Once Patrick had finished all of his sketches and letters, Stan carefully placed them inside his suitcase. The evening of the dance arrived; it was to be held in a dance hall somewhere in Wolverton.

Sarah had been very daring and asked Stan, not to escort her, or anything like that, but to be Percy's guest. Stan was delighted, especially as it meant he could spend some time with Sarah. It was agreed that Thomas would sit with the boys whilst they were at the dance. Simon kept out of the way by going to the pub. He wasn't happy about the arrangement though; in fact, he was seething, and full of resentment towards Stan. He couldn't stand the bloke; he was probably the only one who couldn't wait for him to leave.

Percy had arranged for one of his friends to take Sarah and Stan to the dance. Stan almost wanted to wolf whistle when he saw Sarah. He thought how very beautiful and elegant she looked in her pale blue dress. Matthew looked up at his mum, telling her she looked like Cinderella, from his fairy tales books. "Well, that is a compliment," she said, with a giggle.

Stan felt very proud as he walked into the dance hall with Sarah by his side. He looked around to see where Percy and his wife Judith would be sitting and walked towards their table. There were two other couples sitting at the large table. Percy introduced Stan to them. After lots of hand-shaking, the other couples said how nice it was to meet Stan, saying they had never met an Australian before, and proceeded to ask him lots of questions about Australia.

Stan was delighted to talk about his home country. Stan had noticed a bar in the far corner of the room, where he bought drinks for himself and Sarah, and anyone else at the table who wanted one. Sarah thought he was very generous indeed, although she only asked for a lemonade. Stan was enjoying a beer, he smiled though, as it was rather a warm beer, he was accustomed to ice-cold ones back home.

He had been thinking of home a lot just lately. As his departure was getting very close now, he felt privileged to have met some very nice people whilst he was here, and he would miss them, especially Patrick he thought, and his delightful mother, not to mention Matthew and Thomas, such an outstanding man.

From the stage at the back of the dance hall, the band began to play some dance music, with the couples at their table beginning to sway to the music. Percy was the first one to stand up, offering his hand to Judith; the two of them glided around the dance floor, with Judith looking very striking in her new dress. She looked so petite in Percy's arms; he was just the opposite, being so very large. The two of them were gazing into each other's eyes, still very much in love.

Stan wondered if he should ask Sarah to dance, but decided to wait a while. Sarah looked contented whilst chatting to the other couples before they too stood up to dance. Stan saw his chance and asked if she would like to dance with him. She smiled and took his hand, as he led her onto the dance floor. He took her in his arms.

Instantly, they both felt a deep connection to each other. She could feel Stan's hands on her back, holding her close. His masculinity was obvious to her; she just wanted to melt into him. Looking into his eyes, she could see the tenderness and longing there. As the soft melody of the music continued, so did their desire for each other.

As the music finished, it was replaced by something livelier, both Sarah and Stan smiled at each other, leaving the dance floor and sitting back down at their table again. Sarah was feeling unsure of the intimacy that had passed between them. She knew how attracted they were to each other, but also knew, it was so wrong. At that same moment, the other couples returned to the table, and everyone began to chat with each other again, asking Stan, even more about his life down under as they called it. Towards the end of the evening, the music began to slow down again.

Stan looked at Sarah holding out his hands to her; she shook her head this time.

Oh! How she wanted to be held by him!

Their desire for each other was so strong, but it was just impossible. Stan was disappointed, but understood Sarah, more than she realised. He smiled at her, sitting down contented just to have her nearby. The day had dawned for Stan to start his journey back home. Percy, the ever-available friend, had offered to take Stan and his luggage to Wolverton train station. Everyone had gathered at Thomas's house to say their goodbyes. Firstly, it was little Matthew who wanted to be picked up and cuddled by Stan. Stan happily obliged, gently putting him down again.

Turning to Thomas, he shook his hand, also holding him in a warm embrace, promising to write as soon as he returned home. It was Sarah's turn, he leaned towards her kissing her on the cheek, both not wanting to show their attraction to each other. Patrick stepped forward; they held onto each other for a very long time. Holding Patrick's arms, he gently pushed him away. The weight in Stan's chest felt heavy; this was the hardest thing he had ever had to do. Patrick had meant so much to him for so long; he would never forget his little face the day he found him in the back of his truck.

He told him, "You've grown into a fine young man Patrick. And I've never regretted the day I found you. I wish you nothing but happiness now you're back with your family, and as soon as I get home, I will give Beauty the biggest cuddle you ever did see, telling her, it's sent from you."

With that Patrick smiled, although he felt such sadness, at saying goodbye to this man, who had become like a father to him. Patrick straightened his shoulders trying to be brave and adult. He embraced Stan again, not wanting to let him go.

"I just want to thank you again for everything you have done for me, Stan. Without you, I dread to think of what or where I would have ended up."

Stan held him again saying, "We found each other, that's all that counts, and now you have a great future ahead of you."

With that, Thomas stepped in and with his arm firmly around Patrick, they all said goodbye again, as Stan was driven off in Percy's van. They all waved until the van was out of sight.

Chapter 11

It was now late August, almost two months since Stan had returned to Australia. Patrick had received many letters; some from Stan, and others from Alice; their letters as before were going between them thick and fast, or as fast as the post could go between their two countries. Patrick was so pleased to hear that Beauty was well, and apparently, she still slept at the bottom of Patrick's bed, even though he wasn't there. He thought of Stan every day, and missed him greatly, even though he was now back home and settling in.

Part of him would always be on Stan's property with Beauty, Elijah and Blossom. He often took out the pictures and sketches he had done of Stan's property, just to look at them and remember, especially the almond orchards when they were in blossom; they were such a lovely sight.

Patrick, at fifteen, had officially finished school now, however, he had applied to join an art class, at the nearby college. He was eagerly waiting for their reply, hoping he would be offered a place. Eventually, after waiting for two weeks, he received an acceptance letter. He was thrilled, and so was Sarah. "Well done," she said.

Patrick along with his acceptance letter, peddled his bike across Stony Stratford, to show his granddad.

"Well, I'll be blown," he said, "I'm so pleased for you lad, and it's well deserved." Patrick stayed at his granddad's house for a while longer, before peddling off to show his letter to Robert. Robert was very pleased for Patrick. He had also applied to the same college and received an acceptance letter; he hoped to become an engineer.

With big smiles, the two boys congratulated each other.

Later that evening, at 6 pm prompt, it was supper time. All four of them were sitting around the kitchen table, with a steaming cottage pie in front of them, although, Sarah said, "It's more vegetables than meat," as the rationing was still in place.

Just before Sarah dished up their food, she told Simon all about Patrick's acceptance letter for art college. Simon looked across at Patrick, asking to see the letter. He proudly passed the letter to his father, who looked at it and then tore it into tiny pieces, before throwing it down on the table.

Looking sternly at Patrick, he shouted, "No son of mine is going to a poncy art college," leaving both Sarah and Patrick stunned.

Matthew started to cry. "Oh, for God's sake. All that boy has ever done is cry."

Sarah remarked, "That's because all you ever do is frighten him."

She continued to say, of course, he should go. "Patrick's artwork is wonderful, and his talent should be encouraged and guided at the college."

Simon pushed his chair back and stood up. "Are you deaf or what, Sarah? I said no, and that's the end of it."

He sat down again starting to eat his meal, but no one else wanted theirs. Patrick got up and left the table. Simon called him back. "Do not leave the table, without my say-so, do you hear?" Patrick ignored him and left the house. Sarah went to follow Patrick.

Simon shouted, "That's it, follow him, in case, he gets lost again. Who knows he may end up in Canada this time." He found that very funny, and laughed.

Sarah stopped and turned towards Simon. "What you have just said and done to Patrick is unforgivable. How can you be so cruel to your own son?"

He got up from the table and stood in front of Sarah. "I can say what I like in my own home. And just remember, the army is what's best for him and for Matthew, the cry-baby when he's old enough. Until Patrick is 21, what I say goes, now leave me in peace to eat my supper."

Sarah was shaking with her anger; she quickly took Matthew's hand and left the house to find Patrick. Matthew was still very tearful, but he was pleased to be led away from his father. Sarah thought Patrick might have walked to his granddad's house, but he hadn't gone very far at all. He was standing outside on the pavement, leaning up against the house. She stood next to him still holding Matthew's hand.

"Don't worry, Patrick," she said, "I will make sure you get to college. Now, come on, let's all go back inside."

Patrick went to his room, taking Matthew with him. After making sure the pair of them were alright, Sarah went back into the kitchen. She plated up some food for them taking it upstairs, although she didn't usually encourage eating in their bedrooms, she also didn't want them to be hungry.

Simon was watching her as she was moving around the kitchen. She chose to ignore him and made sure not to make eye contact either. Putting their plates onto a tray, she took the food to the boys. Matthew as always ate heartily; Patrick thanked his mum but just picked at his food.

"Tomorrow," she said, "I will ring the college to sort everything out for you, Patrick, so, please don't worry." Patrick smiled at his mum. She knew her son well and could see he was very troubled by what his father had said. In fact, it had been obvious for some time, to both Sarah and Thomas that Patrick was also missing Stan and his life there.

Since Stan had left to go home, they could see Patrick was torn between his life with them, and his new life in Australia. True to her word, the next morning, Sarah went to the phone box to call the college, unfortunately, her call wasn't answered.

I will have to write a letter instead she thought. Later that day, Patrick visited Robert. He told him briefly what his father had said and done with the college letter. Robert was appalled by what Patrick had told him, "Goodness me," he said, "what a nasty thing to do!"

Patrick explained that his mum was going to write to the college to make sure he was accepted, without needing his father's signature on the college paperwork. After leaving Robert's house, Patrick went to visit his granddad, Sarah and Matthew were already there. Thomas patted Patrick's shoulder as he arrived.

Laughing, he said, "I'm not able to ruffle your hair now, as you've grown so tall that I can't reach!"

Thomas then looked serious, and looking at Patrick he said, "Now, don't you go worrying about that father of yours, your mother and I will make sure everything is sorted out for you. Right then, whose turn is it to feed those pesky chickens of ours?"

A few days later, Matthew was playing in his back garden with an old tennis ball he had found in the tall grass. He was throwing it up against the garden shed and catching it again, missing it a few times. He was starting to become bored, but on his last throw, the ball disappeared behind the shed. Talking to himself, he said, "I had better see if I can reach it."

He looked behind the shed, but he couldn't see where the ball was, the grass was so long and there were stinging nettles. But he could see something glinting in the sunshine; thinking it might be treasure, like in the pirate book he had been reading, he looked around for a stick to dislodge it.

It took him quite a while, but eventually, he pulled out a bottle. He was disappointed; it wasn't treasure after all, just an old bottle. Holding the bottle, he unscrewed the lid and sniffed the liquid inside. He thought it was probably rainwater, but it smelt funny. Knowing his mum collected bottles and jars for her preserves, he took the bottle into the house to show her.

Sarah leaned down and took the bottle from Matthew. "Thank you," she said, "have you had fun playing in the garden?"

Matthew said he had, but could he have a biscuit now and a drink? Laughing Sarah settled him at the kitchen table, before turning her attention back to the bottle.

Like Matthew, she removed the top and sniffed the content, knowing straightaway what it was. She asked Matthew to show her exactly where he had found the bottle.

"In a minute, Mum, I'm just eating my biscuit," he said.

Sarah without asking Simon guessed the vodka bottle belonged to him. *What a stupid person he was* she thought, *to be drinking on top of his medication. No wonder his mood and temper are so bad*. Over the next few days, whilst Simon was at work, Sarah began to check behind the shed. Sure, enough there was always a bottle of vodka hidden there; sometimes, there were two bottles. She didn't want to, but needed to discuss the problem with her dad. Whilst the boys were feeding the chickens, Sarah told him all about the vodka, and how Matthew had innocently found the first bottle. Thomas ran his hands through his thinning hair. "Do you know what?" He said. "I had my suspicions a while ago, but stupidly pushed them to the back of my mind."

Looking at her dad, Sarah said, "It all fits now, that's why his temper has been so bad, and I did notice his words were sometimes slurred, but put it down to the medication he's taking. And he's started to use chewing gum just lately too which he's never done before."

"That would be to mask the smell of the vodka," replied Thomas.

"Oh! What are we going to do now?" She said.

That night, Sarah decided she was going to confront Simon about the vodka. After reading Matthew a chapter from his favourite pirate book, and making sure the boys were asleep, she settled down, waiting anxiously for Simon to come home. He had started to visit the pub after supper; usually, he only went on Sundays.

Hearing him come through the front door, she braced herself. "You're up late," he remarked.

"I'm waiting to speak to you," she replied.

"Oh, yes, and what's that then, need more housekeeping money, do you?"

Smirking he said, "Well, before you ask, the answer is no. Perhaps you could take on more of that sewing you are so fond of."

She never understood why he didn't approve of her sewing; after all, it gave them some extra money, not a great deal, but the extra was always handy. She straightened her shoulders and trying not to look nervous, she mentioned the vodka bottles from behind the garden shed.

His mouth hung open. Thinking quickly, he said, "So, you and that old dad of yours have put two and two together, and blamed me."

"This has nothing to do with my dad, Simon, and you know that."

She went on to tell him about the first bottle, being found by Matthew playing in the garden.

"Oh, so, he plays behind the shed now, does he? Was he crying again?"

She ignored that remark. "I was concerned, Simon, so I've been looking behind the shed most days and found quite a few bottles of vodka."

"Well, congratulations," he said, "quite the detective, aren't you?"

"I was thinking," she said, "perhaps you should see the doctor again, maybe your medication needs some attention, then you won't need the alcohol."

Raising his voice, he said, "Don't you tell me what I need. What the hell do you know anyway?"

Sarah had never felt so uncomfortable with Simon before; he had become like a stranger to her. "Simon," she pleaded, "please be sensible, it isn't good for you to mix your tablets with vodka, I just want to help you that's all."

He looked at her as if he hated her. She flinched thinking he was about to strike her. Instead, he walked away shouting over his shoulder, "You're pathetic, did you know that? And come to think of it, those two boys are just like you, pathetic." With that, he left the house again. She didn't know where he had gone but guessed it was to retrieve his vodka.

Life continued for them in Church Street. Matthew started his new school and was enjoying it, especially his school dinners. Every afternoon after school, he would tell whoever wanted to listen, exactly what he had eaten for his dinner. Patrick had begun his college course and was enjoying that too. Every day he called for Robert, just like before, catching the bus into Wolverton together. That particular evening, they had made plans to go to the youth club.

Patrick didn't realise it, but he was of great interest to Robert's sisters, Maggie and Hazel. As Patrick and Robert entered the youth club that evening, they were immediately joined by Maggie and Hazel, which annoyed Robert.

He told them to clear off. He just wanted to enjoy the evening with himself and Patrick, giggling both girls each linked their arms through Patrick's. Looking sternly at his sister's, Robert said again, "Just clear off or else we won't come here again."

Patrick was starting to feel embarrassed by their attention. Eventually, they removed their arms from Patrick's and walked off giggling as they went. They both thought thank goodness for that and got on with enjoying the rest of their evening.

Maggie and Hazel though were watching Patrick all evening. Simon was pleased to be at work, away from Sarah's prying eyes. He was furious she had suggested he should see a doctor, who the hell did she think she was?

It wasn't her! That had been fighting in the war, oh no! There she was safely at home, with just a baby to look after, whilst he was away fighting, no wonder he needed a drink.

After dealing with a couple of meat deliveries, he drove off heading for a secluded place he had found where he had hidden some vodka. He pulled over onto a dirt road. Getting out of the van, he walked towards a dead tree. It had been struck by lightning many years ago, leaving a large hollow in the tree trunk. Smiling to himself and licking his lips in anticipation, he felt inside the tree trunk for his bottle of vodka.

Lifting the bottle up to his lips, he drank heavily again and again. Slumping against the tree, he took another gulp, before carefully replacing the bottle. Walking unsteadily back to the delivery van, he drove away.

He had three more deliveries to do and hoped to cover the ground as quickly as he could so that he could stop on the way back for another drink. His dependency was becoming all-consuming. He put his foot down heavily on the accelerator, driving off towards the village of Wicken. He knew full well the roads in that area were very narrow. But he didn't care, he was thinking of Sarah, and how much she had annoyed him the previous day, which made him drive even faster. Knowing the roads in that area were usually quiet, he sped along without a care in the world. Unfortunately for Simon, he had forgotten about the sharp corner up ahead. As he rounded a corner, his tyres hit a grass verge, making the vehicle skid, he gripped the steering wheel, trying to stop the van from veering off the road. But the van was out of control; there was a sickening thud as the van collided with a tree.

Simon lay unconscious his head against the windscreen, with blood pouring down his face. At home, Sarah thought it was strange; Simon was usually home by now, maybe he had decided to visit the pub. By going to the pub, he probably thought it would annoy her, he didn't agree with seeing a doctor again. Simon was late returning to the butcher's shop that evening.

So, Percy called around to their house, thinking maybe Simon had gone home for a while before returning the van back to the butcher's shop. Sarah asked Percy to come inside. She told him Simon was always home for supper by 6 pm, and it was odd that he wasn't; maybe he decided to visit the pub on the way, she said and got delayed.

Percy looked thoughtful, knowing Simon usually parked the van outside the butcher's shop, and always went inside, along with the day's takings, before going anywhere else.

Percy said, "Maybe he's had a puncture or some engine trouble. I had better drive out that way, and see what's happened." With that, he left.

Percy drove back to his butcher's shop to tell Judith he was going to look for Simon. But just as he was getting into his car, a police car pulled up outside his shop. Percy was concerned; he stepped out, asking them if he could help. He asked them inside his shop, turning to them with a worried look; he asked them again how he could help. The officers informed him of the accident they had been called out to.

Saying how sorry they were, but Simon couldn't be saved. Percy put his head in his hands. "Oh God! That poor family," he said, Judith had heard every word and started to cry. Percy told them where Simon's family lived, the officers left his shop with heavy hearts. Percy thought he had better fetch Thomas, his daughter would need him. Leaving Judith, he set off for Thomas's house. Thomas opened the door to Percy, saying, "This is a nice surprise," until he saw his ashen face. "Whatever is the matter?" He asked.

"I'm afraid there has been an accident, Thomas. You're needed at Sarah's house." With that, Percy went back to his car. Thomas followed him but didn't ask anything else.

Sarah was in shock, and so were Patrick and Matthew, although Matthew didn't fully understand. Percy took the boys back to his shop for a while, leaving the police to talk with Sarah and Thomas. Thomas sat beside Sarah holding her hand, whilst the police were with them. They told her quietly how Simon had died instantly. However, a full investigation would take place. But they were sorry to say it looked like Simon had taken the corner too fast, losing control of the van.

Chapter 12

Many months had gone by and it was nearly Christmas again. Sarah was determined to make sure the boys had a good time. They spent Christmas Day and Boxing Day at Thomas's house.

On Boxing Day, they were joined by Percy and his wife, Judith, bringing with them some gifts for the boys; art things for Patrick, and adventure books for Matthew. Sarah was very grateful to them both. They had been a tower of strength to them all, especially after what happened to Simon. Everyone found themselves sitting at the table for a game of Monopoly.

Unfortunately, Matthew kept finding himself in jail, which he wasn't very pleased about. He sulked for a while, before telling everyone he would prefer to play snakes and ladders instead!

Later, the adults sat in more comfortable chairs, each with a drink in their hand; their conversation turning to Patrick and Australia. It was one subject Patrick loved to talk about. He still missed his life there, and everyone he knew, he wrote as often as he could to Stan and Alice, never forgetting to ask after Beauty, and also Elijah and Blossom.

Percy thought for a while and said, "Why don't you go for a holiday, Patrick?"

He smiled at that, knowing full well he hardly had any money. He did have a Saturday job in a shoe shop, but he didn't earn a great deal. It would take him several years to save up.

Percy went on to say, "I think you should all go, it will do you the world of good, put the past behind you!"

Thomas was listening and thinking maybe they could have a holiday in Australia. Once the Christmas period was over, Thomas asked Percy if he wouldn't mind giving him a lift to see his bank manager.

"Now, you've put the seed in my head about Australia, Percy, I want to discuss it with my bank manager. I know how much money I have saved up, but I could do with some financial advice as well."

Percy said, "You old codger you! I bet you have loads stashed away for a rainy day."

It was now January, a new year in Stony Stratford. Thomas had decided he would send his family to visit Stan in Australia. He was aware of how torn Patrick was between his family here, and that great big country he had also come to love.

The letters between Patrick, Stan and Alice were still travelling thick and fast.

I'm getting old he thought, *and don't need the money, but it would be lovely to see the look on their faces when he told them of his plans.*

Later that day, with it being a Sunday, Sarah, Patrick and Matthew were all going to their granddad's house for tea.

They arrived at 3 pm, all wrapped up against the cold day. After removing their coats, hats and scarves, everyone was grateful for the warmth from the fire, which was roaring away in the hearth. Thomas went into the kitchen to make them all a warming drink.

There was lots of chatter, especially from Matthew, compared to Patrick at that age. He was a very talkative little boy. He asked his granddad if he had any nice biscuits too.

Sarah told him off. "You should wait to be offered one," she said, "it's rude to ask."

Matthew just grinned and said, "But I'm hungry, Mum!"

Laughing together, they chorused, "You're always hungry."

Looking at them all, Thomas cleared his throat; looking very serious he said, "There's something I want to talk to you all about." Everyone looked at him, waiting for him to speak.

He wasn't sure of how to say it, so he just blurted out, "You're all going to have a holiday in Australia."

Sarah was speechless, so was Patrick, and Matthew hadn't a clue where Australia was.

"What do you mean, Dad?" Sarah asked.

With a huge smile on his face, Thomas said, "Well, now I know how much Patrick misses Stan, not forgetting Alice," he said, with a wink at Patrick, "making him blush."

Thomas continued to say, "I have the means to pay for you to have a holiday of a lifetime."

"Oh, Granddad," said Patrick, "you really don't need to do that; it would cost such a lot."

His granddad leaned forward, saying, "But I want to do it, lad." Sarah knew her dear dad would have given this decision a lot of thought, although she was still shocked. She asked, "Will you be coming with us, Dad?"

"No," he said, "I'm far too old, for all that travelling."

Sarah gave this some thought, before saying, "But, Dad you are only 65, that isn't old. We're all so grateful to you, but I wouldn't dream of going without you."

Thomas had already discussed his plans with Percy, however, the next time Percy called to see him, Thomas told him what Sarah had said. Percy replied, "Well, she's right! Why don't you go with them, Thomas?"

"But I'm 65," he repeated.

"All the more reason to go then, you only live once. I'm 50 myself and would jump at the chance."

Thomas pondered the thought for over a week, before making his decision. The boys and Sarah were jubilant at Thomas's decision to go with them.

Sarah hugged her dad. "Oh, what would we ever do without you?" She said.

Patrick was thoughtful, saying it wouldn't be wise to visit Stan at harvest time, knowing what a busy time the almond harvest would be. After lots of discussion, they settled on August, although it seemed a long time to wait.

It would fit in better for the college and school term times. Matthew pipped up to everyone, he wouldn't mind missing school, but he would miss his school dinners. Everyone laughed at that, which Matthew thought very strange, as he was quite serious about his dinners. Patrick had written to Cecily in Bathurst, telling her of their plans. She was delighted and promised to keep it a secret from Stan. Patrick so wanted to surprise him.

They had been making plans for their journey for months, and finally, August had arrived. Robert had offered to look after Thomas's chickens and promised to feed them every day. Percy had arranged for a local man to tend both Thomas and Sarah's gardens for them whilst they were away as well. The day arrived. It started at Wolverton train station, waving them off from the station platform, were Percy and Judith. Hours later, they all arrived rather tired, except for Patrick at Tilbury docks.

There, in front of them stood the ship. Looking up, Sarah said, "My goodness, it's a large ship."

They very soon found themselves settled into their cabin. They had picked a family cabin which had a small porthole, where they could see the waves splashing about. It wasn't long before the ship sailed from Tilbury, and they were on their way.

"My, my, you were correct, Patrick, I can't even feel the ship moving," said Thomas. Patrick secretly hoped there wouldn't be a storm to upset his granddad. Everyone thoroughly enjoyed the voyage. Matthew as usual, particularly enjoyed the food on offer. It was the wonderful sea views enjoyed by everyone else. Whilst Patrick was sitting on the top deck along with his granddad, he asked if he was enjoying his journey.

"Oh, yes," he said, "it's marvellous and I'm so pleased to be with you all."

Looking at the ocean below, "Isn't it amazing," said Patrick, "and so very blue, but at the same time it's almost aqua, and when we get closer to any land, it changes to turquoise."

Thomas looked at the young man next to him, thinking what an amazing eye he had for colours. Patrick went on to tell his granddad that he hoped to see an albatross; he wasn't lucky enough on his last voyage.

"In that case, I will keep an eye out for one too."

Their voyage continued with everyone enjoying every minute. Patrick spent a lot of time on the top deck, painting the various ocean scenes in front of him; his artistic eye not missing anything. Patrick told them all not to miss seeing the sky at night it was stunning. So, before turning in for the night, all four of them stood on the top deck, with Patrick, looking up towards the night sky, and sure enough, it was breathtaking. The stars were twinkling against the inky black sky, merging down into the ocean below.

"It's so beautiful," said Sarah. The view brought tears to Thomas's eyes. They were beginning to get closer to Australia now, and the temperature was warming up.

In the morning whilst Thomas and Patrick were settled on the deck again, Sarah took Matthew to play Quoits. It was a game he had come to enjoy; he also played hopscotch with some of the other children. Sarah was watching him smiling at his antics. Up on the deck, Thomas nudged Patrick urgently. "Look," he said. Patrick looked to where his granddad was pointing. "It's an albatross."

"Oh, wow!" said Patrick. He could hardly believe his eyes, there it was, the bird he had hoped to see. Straining his neck to watch as the bird soared and glided on the thermals. Patrick was amazed; it looked so majestic up there, in the wide blue sky.

As the albatross disappeared from view, Patrick quickly picked up his sketchbook and began to sketch what he had just witnessed. Today, the ship docked in Sydney. From the deck above, Patrick was scanning the faces of the people below; he was looking for Alice. And there she was, looking back up at him. Laughing he waved, with Alice frantically waving back. Standing with her, were her parents, Cecily and Jeff, and the twins Ronnie and James. Patrick pointed them out to his mum and granddad, not forgetting Matthew.

When Patrick eventually came face to face in front of Alice, he could hardly believe it. They held onto each other, for a long time. Patrick then embraced both Cecily and Jeff, before he remembered to introduce his family to them.

There was lots of smiling and hand-shaking, before they all left Sydney, for Bathurst. Jeff had borrowed a minibus; Patrick sat in the back seat with Alice. He marvelled at how Alice had changed; she had grown into a lovely young woman, he thought, however, she still had the merriment he remembered. Her hair was now long and held back in a ponytail; her eyes were still blue and sparkling as he remembered.

Finally, having just one stop, they arrived at Cecily and Jeff's home. After having some refreshments, the whole family wanted to show them around their property. Thomas was surprised at the vastness of it all. Laughing, Patrick said, "You've seen nothing yet, Granddad," thinking of Stan's place.

Alice proudly took them over to the stables, where she brought out Midnight her horse. Both Alice and Patrick had remembered his many disastrous horse riding lessons. They spent three very enjoyable days at Cecily and Jeff's home, before leaving again in the minibus, for Stan's property.

Patrick explained to his mum and granddad that it was a long journey, he asked his granddad how he was coping.

"I'm just fine, lad," he said, "couldn't be better."

Sarah was taking in the wonderful views. She was aware it was a large country, but she hadn't expected it to be so beautiful. Matthew had become best friends with the twins,

Ronnie and James. They had their heads together chatting all of the time.

Knowing their interest in racing cars, Mathew couldn't help boasting that he lived very close to Silverstone, but he had to admit, he hadn't ever been there. But he said he would when he got home, then he would write to them all about it. Again, Patrick and Alice were sitting in the back of the minibus, talking ten to the dozen, trying to catch up for their lost years. Sarah was listening to them, and was worried; Patrick seemed animated here in this country. She hoped he didn't want to stay, and wondered how she would cope with that.

This time, they needed two stops before reaching the outskirts of Gilgandra. Patrick kept asking both his mum and granddad if they were alright. Like Sarah, Thomas was enjoying the journey immensely. Through the minibus windows, Thomas noticed the beautiful birds. He asked if they were parrots.

"They are parrots," replied Cecily, turning around from the front seat. "Look," she said, "there's some Galahs as well."

Thomas and Sarah had never seen birds quite like this before. Patrick informed them, "As we get closer to Stan's, it will become very rural, and you will probably see some kangaroos."

"What about a koala?" Matthew said wanting to join in.

Patrick told him he had only ever seen one of those once, and that was back in Bathurst when he visited a zoo, explaining they were shy animals, and also very hard to spot, Matthew seemed content with that.

Sure enough, as they drew very near to Stan's place, they saw the kangaroos hopping along in their habitat. Again, both Thomas and Sarah were in wonder at everything they saw.

Stan and Elijah were relaxing on Stan's veranda whilst enjoying a cool beer. Beauty was lying stretched out in the shade next to Stan. They were talking together about the previous harvest, and how well it had gone, although their working days were very long. Stan was also discussing he wanted to invest in more almond trees, adding to his orchard, maybe around one hundred he said.

Elijah was about to respond when Beauty started to bark. She stood up on all fours, looking towards their front gates. Stan smiled, saying there were probably some kangaroos nearby; she had never lost the habit of barking at kangaroos.

Beauty ran off at full speed towards their front gates. Stan called her back, but she wasn't listening that's for sure.
Blossom came out of her house, wanting to know what all the barking was about. She was barking for the entire world to hear. Stan soon realised what all the fuss was about; in the distance, he could see a vehicle approaching his property.

I wonder who that could be he thought. Both Stan Elijah and Blossom, watched as the vehicle approached. Elijah, at a nod from Stan, opened the gates for the minibus to come through. Still, Beauty was barking like never before. As the minibus drew to a halt, with a huge smile on his face, Patrick stepped out. Beauty jumped at him, nearly knocking him over, such was her joy.

Patrick's clothes were covered in dust from her paws; laughing, he hugged her close to him. She continued to jump around him, her tail wagging with excitement and pleasure.

"Well, I never!" said Stan, as he pulled Patrick towards him, holding him in a warm embrace. Elijah, with a wide smile, slapped him on the back, pumping his hand at the same time. Blossom held out her arms with teary eyes, holding him tightly. From the minibus, Sarah was brought to tears watching their reunion. Still watching them, she looked towards Stan, and her heart missed a beat.